The
Nutcracker
Mice

The Nutcracker Mice

KRISTIN KLADSTRUP
illustrated by Brett Helquist

CANDLEWICK PRESS

Text copyright © 2017 by Kristin Kladstrup
Illustrations copyright © 2017 by Brett Helquist

First paperback edition 2020

Library of Congress Catalog Card Number 2017957433
ISBN 978-0-7636-8519-5 (hardcover)
ISBN 978-1-5362-1576-2 (paperback)

20 21 22 23 24 25 TRC 10 9 8 7 6 5 4 3 2 1

Printed in Eagan, MN, USA

This book was typeset in Caslon.
The illustrations were done in oil and acrylic.

Candlewick Press
99 Dover Street
Somerville, Massachusetts 02144

www.candlewick.com

For Tommy
K. K.

For Regina and Eva
B. H.

THE NUTCRACKER
A Ballet in Two Acts

with music by
Pyotr Ilyich Tchaikovsky

*Mariinsky Theater * Saint Petersburg * December 1892*

Scenario

ACT I

The Silberhaus family is having a Christmas party. As the Christmas tree is decorated, guests arrive and enjoy refreshments. The children, including Fritz and Clara Silberhaus, are invited into the room to enjoy the festivities.

When Fritz and Clara's godfather, a man named Drosselmayer, arrives, he brings presents, including a nutcracker. Fritz and Clara quarrel over the nutcracker, and Fritz breaks its jaw. Saddened, Clara comforts the nutcracker.

Meanwhile, the guests dance.

When bedtime arrives, Clara wants to take the nutcracker with her. Her request is denied. The children leave the party. The guests depart, the Silberhaus parents retire, and the house is quiet.

Clara returns to look at the nutcracker. Suddenly, the room is invaded by mice. Frightened, Clara watches as the Christmas tree grows large. Dolls and other toys and gingerbread soldiers come to life. A battle ensues, and the mice overcome and eat the gingerbread soldiers.

Clara's nutcracker also comes to life and takes command of an army of tin soldiers. As the battle grows fierce, the mouse king arrives and faces off with the nutcracker. Clara throws her shoe at the mouse king, and the nutcracker and his army are the victors.

The nutcracker is transformed into a prince. Hand in hand, he and Clara walk into the branches of the Christmas tree. They find themselves in a forest of fir trees. Dancing snowflakes waltz in the moonlight.

ACT II

In a fantastic Kingdom of Sweets, the Sugar Plum Fairy and her consort await the arrival of Clara and the nutcracker prince. The Sugar Plum Fairy provides entertainments that include Spanish, Arabian, Chinese, and Russian dances, performing clowns, dancing flutes, and a "Waltz of the Flowers." The Sugar Plum Fairy and her consort perform a *grand pas de deux*. After a final waltz, the ballet comes to a dazzling conclusion in the Kingdom of Sweets.

CHAPTER 1

Not a Very Good Story

THERE WERE MICE at the Mariinsky.

Saint Petersburg's famous theater—home to the world's most spectacular ballets—was completely overrun by creatures that Irina's father jokingly called *the world's tiniest balletomanes.*

"I think the mice really do love the ballet," Irina told Papa one evening.

"Well, if they don't, they ought to!" he said. "All Russians love ballet, and they are Russian mice, after all."

Irina was aware that her father was teasing her. She said, "But I saw the mice. They were peeking out from the carvings on the front of the tsar's box. A whole crowd of them watching *The Sleeping Beauty*."

Irina was nine years old, and had not only seen *The Sleeping Beauty* but had also been to any number of its rehearsals. She even knew some of the performers. That was because her father and mother worked at the Mariinsky Theater. Papa was the chief custodian, and Mama was a seamstress in the costume department. Mama had stitched the skirt on the dress worn by the Lilac Fairy in *The Sleeping Beauty*, and Irina had helped her.

"More likely the mice were there for the crumbs left after one of the parties in the tsar's salon," said Papa.

The tsar, who enjoyed the ballet as much as any other citizen of Saint Petersburg, often held parties in a special room behind the royal box. There were cakes and pastries; Papa and the other custodians always had to clean up afterward.

"But they *are* clever mice," Irina insisted.

"No doubt about that! They've outwitted every mousetrap I've ever set for them," said Papa, who, as chief custodian, was expected to get rid of the mice. Not that he had ever succeeded in catching a single one.

Irina said, "If they're clever, they *might* like the ballet! Do you know what I think, Papa? I think the mice might like to dance!"

"Well, I suppose they might."

Her father was humoring her. He didn't really believe that the mice could dance, but Irina had her own secret reason for believing that they could. She said, "I mean it, Papa. They might listen to the orchestra and dance somewhere out of sight. Under the stage, maybe."

He chuckled. "They might have their own ballet company, eh?"

"Why not?" For the secret reason mentioned above, Irina had lately been thinking quite a bit about the Mariinsky mice.

Papa said, "I expect the mice will like the new ballet the theater is putting on."

Irina knew which ballet he meant; it was one that no one had ever seen before. It was called *The Nutcracker*, and it would be shown at Christmastime. That was months away, but Irina's mother and the other seamstresses were already busy sewing the costumes: dresses for a party in the first act, dresses for dancing snowflakes, and dresses of golden cloth for the "Waltz of the Flowers" in the second act. Papa had read aloud to Irina the story that had inspired the new ballet—all about a nutcracker, who was really a prince, and a vengeful mouse king leading an army of mice.

Irina had enjoyed the story, but recalling it now, she frowned. The mice in it had been such mean-tempered, nasty creatures. "Oh, but Papa! I don't think the Mariinsky mice will like the new ballet."

"What's that? Why not?"

At that moment Irina felt as if she were a mouse; she felt tiny and powerless and indignant about the unfair opinion people had of her. She felt angry with her father for setting all the mousetraps at the theater, even if it *was* his job to do so.

"Really, Papa," she said, not hiding her disapproval. "If you're a mouse, *The Nutcracker* is not a very good story at all!"

CHAPTER 2

Lard and Stale Bread

SNAP! THE SHARP-TOOTHED jaws of the mousetrap clamped shut. Esmeralda felt her tail twitch and her heart thump. She said, "I will never get used to this."

"Never mind," said her twin brother, Gringoire. "These new traps are no more a danger to us than the old ones, now that we know how to disarm them."

The two mice stood at a safe distance from the mousetrap at the top of the stairs that led to the attic of the Mariinsky Theater. It was Gringoire who had figured out how to toss a kopek into the trap. The coin jarred the mechanism, setting it off, so the mice could safely retrieve the bait. There were mousetraps like this one all over the theater, and all the Mariinsky mice knew how to use Gringoire's trick.

"We're lucky we got here before anybody else," said Gringoire. There were quite a few mice who made their home in the attic, but the siblings had risen early in the hope of finding something for breakfast. Esmeralda climbed over the tightly shut jaws, shuddering at the touch of the cold metal. She picked up the kopek and handed it to her brother. Then she scraped up the morsel of lard from the metal tongue in the center of the trap. The morsel was smaller than a hazelnut, hardly enough for one mouse, let alone two.

Or three. Their cousin usually joined them for meals. "Maybe Conrad will have brought something back from scrounge patrol last night," said Esmeralda as they made their way across the attic floor to her brother's home.

The scrounge patrols were a necessity of life at the Mariinsky. The mousetraps had never provided enough to eat, so from time to time, teams of volunteers would venture outside for additional provisions, which were then turned over to a special committee of mice who stockpiled the food at several locations within the walls of the theater. The food could then be parceled out to families, but patrol members, who risked dogs, cats, rats, and other dangers in the alleys, streets, and squares of Saint Petersburg, were usually rewarded with extra provisions for their efforts. Esmeralda had recently passed the birthday that marked her as an adult, which meant that she would soon go out on scrounge patrol.

Conrad was waiting for them as they rounded the corner of a wooden crate. "Lard again, I see," he commented. "Lucky for us I managed to wrest this fresh bread away from a gang of outlaw rats."

He was joking. The crust of bread he had for them wasn't fresh. Nor, Esmeralda knew, had he actually taken it from rats. Conrad would be the first to admit that he was a timid soul. He would no more seek out a rat gang than a cat, which meant that his offerings from scrounge patrol were generally the things that were easiest to find. All the same, stale bread was better than no bread.

She gave her cousin a hug. "We have all the makings of a feast!" she said. "But we'll have to eat quickly if we're to get to class on time."

The class she would be attending with Conrad was the daily practice for the Russian Mouse Ballet Company. Though Esmeralda had only recently been accepted into the *corps de ballet,* she had been given an important role in an upcoming production. She was eager to measure up to the expectations of the company's ballet mistress, Madame Giselle.

Conrad divided the bread into three pieces, and Gringoire smeared lard on each one. The mice ate in silence until Esmeralda asked, "Did you get in very late, Conrad?"

"Not so very," he said as he cleaned his whiskers. They were black, which gave him a rakish appearance that was much appreciated by Esmeralda's friends in the *corps de ballet*. Conrad was one of the company's principal dancers, and Esmeralda was always being pressed by her fellow ballerinas to give information about her handsome cousin. "I got more sleep than usual," he went on, "which is good, since Madame Giselle has got me down for an afternoon rehearsal *and* an evening rehearsal with Fleur."

Fleur de Lys was the *prima ballerina* of the Russian Mouse Ballet Company; she had starred in its last two productions.

"Rehearsals for *The Nutcracker*?" said Gringoire.

Conrad made a face. "Yes, more's the pity."

"You don't sound too happy."

"Who could be? The scenario is terrible. You never heard such a dreadful story!"

Gringoire looked surprised. "What's wrong with it? I thought it was based on Hoffmann's *The Nutcracker and the Mouse King*. That's a wonderful story!"

Though Esmeralda's brother often helped out with the ballet company's productions, he was not a dancer. When he was younger, Gringoire had ventured into one of the theater offices to nibble a pastry left out on a desk. Marius Petipa, ballet master at the Mariinsky, had come upon him unexpectedly. Esmeralda's brother had escaped through a hole in the wall, but not before Monsieur Petipa had brought his brass-tipped walking stick down on Gringoire's hind leg. He still walked with a limp that prevented him from dancing and, for that matter, from scrounge patrol duty.

Not that Gringoire ever complained. He often remarked that his injury was a blessing in disguise, for it allowed him to devote countless hours to his favorite pastime of reading. All the Mariinsky mice could read both Russian and French; they attended classes as children so they could read the theater programs. But Gringoire adored books, and for this reason his home was tucked in among several tall stacks of them that someone had left in the attic. There was a French retelling of *The Nutcracker and the Mouse King* among the books in his collection; Gringoire had read it aloud to Esmeralda. She hadn't liked it as much as her brother had. Some of the characters were decidedly unappealing; in addition to the wicked mouse king, there was a nasty mouse queen and a fickle-hearted princess named Pirlipat. Esmeralda was relieved these last two had been left out of the ballet. She said, "It's nothing like the story you read me, Gringoire. Monsieur Petipa and Monsieur Vsevolozhsky have changed everything!"

Ivan Alexandrovich Vsevolozhsky was the director of the imperial theaters in Russia, and

Esmeralda suspected that it was he who had come up with the scenario for the new ballet. The man seemed to have his hand in everything that went on at the Mariinsky.

Conrad said, "Everyone's upset about the battle scene in the first act. The mouse king and his army show up for no reason whatsoever and they all get killed."

"The other characters in the ballet are supposed to rejoice about that," Esmeralda explained. "You know—because they're pretending to be humans. But it's hard to pretend to be joyful about mice getting killed!"

"The audience certainly won't like it," said Conrad.

Gringoire said, "All the same, the battle does sound dramatic."

"Too bad it's the only dramatic thing in the ballet," said Conrad. "The second act is just a lot of candy and other nonsense."

Esmeralda wondered if her cousin wasn't being too harsh. She did love the score for the ballet. The music had been composed by Tchaikovsky, the same man who had written the score for the Mariinsky Theater's recent production of *The Sleeping Beauty*. She said, "The 'Dance of the Sugar Plum Fairy' is pretty. And the 'Waltz of the Flowers' is lovely."

Conrad gave a snort. "But nothing *happens*! If the audience hasn't left at intermission, they'll fall asleep."

The audience would be the ballet-loving mice of Saint Petersburg, and the performance would take place, as did all performances by the Russian Mouse Ballet Company, in a space behind the stage where the human dancers performed. The space had been a closet, once upon a time, before a wall was put up, sealing it off. Thankfully, the wall had not sealed off the sounds of the human orchestra. The mouse audience could hear perfectly well as they watched the mouse performers dance atop a stage made from a shallow box that had been left in the old closet. The mice even had some light from candle stubs they had brought in through tunnels in the walls. It took three so-called *fire-mice* to light a single match and touch it to each of the candlewicks in turn. The fire-mice also kept watch over the candles in case they went out during a performance. And, in case of fire, they stood by with an array of walnut shells filled with water.

"Is anybody worried that you might not even have an audience?" asked Gringoire.

Esmeralda and Conrad winced at this blunt question. The truth was that the most recent ballets presented by the Russian Mouse Ballet Company had not been successful. An illness had swept through the colony of mice living in the theater a few years back. Many talented dancers, including Esmeralda and Gringoire's parents, had died. The company's remaining principal dancers and soloists weren't quite as strong as their predecessors. Conrad was an exception; his talent and good looks made him popular with audiences. But Fleur de Lys, though technically proficient, had yet to inspire the same adoration as the *prima ballerina* before her.

Moreover, the Russian Mouse Ballet Company had increasingly found itself competing with the human ballet company. This competition was not new; it had always been the case that the mouse balletomanes of Saint Petersburg would occasionally take in one of the human productions at the Mariinsky. The mice could sneak into the theater and watch the human stage from holes cleverly hidden in the carved fronts of the theater loges. What had changed was that the human productions had become so elaborate. First, there was *The Sleeping Beauty*, with its gorgeous score by Tchaikovsky and its beautiful scenery and costumes. The mice had danced to the same music, of course, but Madame Giselle had insisted that they didn't need costumes or sets. "It is the dancing that matters. Monsieur Petipa's production of the ballet is nothing but spectacle!"

Madame Giselle was not alone in her assessment of Monsieur Petipa's production of *The Sleeping Beauty;* a number of human critics had made similar complaints in the Saint Petersburg newspapers. Audiences, however, didn't seem to mind. People had flocked to Monsieur Petipa's spectacular production in droves.

People . . . and mice. Indeed, the Saint Petersburg mice had preferred Monsieur Petipa's production of *The Sleeping Beauty* to such a degree that, by its close, audiences for the mouse production had dwindled away to a few loyal fans.

The Sleeping Beauty had been followed by another lavish ballet. Monsieur Petipa's production of this one had featured some two hundred dancers, a golden chariot drawn by horses, and an elephant. Small wonder that the unadorned mouse production had closed after only three performances.

Indeed, it was due to the Russian Mouse Ballet Company's failure to attract audiences that the Mariinsky mice now spent even more time than usual hunting for food. Their Saint Petersburg audiences had always paid for admission to the mouse ballets with crusts of bread, chopped nuts, bits of cheese, and even cookies and cakes. Now, with so many mice choosing to watch Monsieur Petipa's dancers (*for free,* as Conrad pointed out), the Mariinsky mice had no recourse but to scrounge for food outside. Stale bread, usually—and never quite enough.

"Of course we're worried," said Conrad. "We've got dancers spending their nights hunting for food. They're tired and not up to practicing during the day. Everyone's trying because we all know we've got to win back our audience. But once word gets out that the scenario for *The Nutcracker* is offensive to mice, who knows if anybody will show up to see it?"

"Do you think word *will* get out?" Esmeralda asked anxiously.

"It always does—especially when you have mice like Franz spreading rumors."

Franz had been a soloist with the Russian Mouse Ballet Company until a mousetrap had snipped off a portion of his tail. The injury had affected his dancing, and he had been knocked down into the *corps de ballet.* Embittered by this demotion, he was always complaining and gossiping. If he was talking to mice outside the Mariinsky, it couldn't be good.

Conrad said, "Even Madame Giselle is worried about the *Nutcracker* scenario."

Esmeralda gave a start. It hadn't occurred to her that the ballet mistress might be worried. Only last week, Madame Giselle had said, "This is the perfect ballet for you, Esmeralda! I predict that we may have a new *prima ballerina* after the audience sees you in the role of Clara."

The role of Clara was perfect for Esmeralda for one very important reason. But what would that matter if nobody came to see *The Nutcracker*? Esmeralda said, "There must be something we can do!"

Conrad licked a last trace of lard from his hand. "Short of performing a completely different ballet, I'd say we're doomed. But that can't stop us from practicing. Come on, Esmeralda, or we'll be late for class."

CHAPTER 3

The Training Ribbon

DESPITE THE GLOOMY prospects for *The Nutcracker*, Esmeralda felt her spirits rise at class that morning. She grasped the barre—a length of twine stretched between the stud nails behind one of the walls of the Mariinsky—and followed the movements of the line of dancers in front of her. *Demi-plié, grand plié, tendu, relevé, rond-de-jambe . . .* With each movement, Esmeralda reveled in the command her mind held over her body. How easy it was to keep the count for the *grand battement en cloche*! She raised her left leg, stretching it high:

forward on the count of one, backward on the count of two, forward and backward again, like the clapper on a bell.

Madame Giselle always held her morning class at the same time as the humans held theirs. Small holes in the wall, carefully hidden around the full-length mirrors in the human rehearsal room on the other side, ensured that the mice had light for their practice. They also had music. Just now the human rehearsal pianist was playing a rather tinny-sounding march, more militant than lyrical; all the same, it was easy for Esmeralda to imagine that she was on stage, dancing to the uplifting music from *The Sleeping Beauty.* She held her head erect, letting her arm trail through the air like a wisp of smoke.

Meanwhile, Madame Giselle strolled up and down the line of dancers, scrutinizing their movements. Sometimes she praised. More often she criticized. Which was only right: like Monsieur Petipa, Madame Giselle was French and had high standards. She had come to the Mariinsky inside the carpetbag of a visiting Parisian ballerina. Although the ballerina had left soon after arriving, complaining that the Russian winter was unbearably cold, Madame Giselle, inspired by the fiery enthusiasm of the Saint Petersburg balletomanes, had decided to stay on as ballet mistress of the Russian Mouse Ballet Company. "We must reward the audience with our very best performance," she was always declaring.

Now Esmeralda sensed that Madame Giselle was watching *her*. Surely it was impossible to improve her extension. Still, Esmeralda made every effort to do so, stretching her leg high in what she hoped was a perfect *développé à la seconde*.

She was rewarded. "*Très bien*, Esmeralda! The training ribbon is helping you maintain the correct position of your tail."

Though Esmeralda felt pleased, she did wish that the ballet mistress would not draw attention

to the lavender-colored ribbon looped about her tail and tied around her waist. The ribbon kept her tail in the proper ballet position: wrapped tightly around her body. Keeping one's tail in position without the use of a training ribbon was not easy; it tended to hinder one's movement and make one feel rather stiff. It was common for children in Madame Giselle's ballet school to wear training ribbons. The problem was that Esmeralda was not a child. Nor was she a beginning dancer. She was a member of the Russian Mouse Ballet Company. None of the other dancers in the company needed to use a training ribbon, and it was a source of enormous frustration to Esmeralda that she did.

It was a source of frustration for Madame Giselle as well. "I do not understand why you have such trouble with your tail, Esmeralda. You come from a long line of truly great dancers."

This was true. Esmeralda's grandfather had founded the Russian Mouse Ballet Company, serving as its first ballet master. Esmeralda's grandmother had been its first *prima ballerina,* making her name dancing the difficult lead roles in *Giselle* and *Coppélia.* Esmeralda's parents had both been soloists, and now her cousin was the company's most popular principal dancer. The only thing that Esmeralda could think was that her tail must somehow be constructed differently from the tails of everyone else in her family!

"You bring such a lovely emotional quality to your dancing," Madame Giselle had told her. "Your technique is always excellent. The only thing that keeps you from becoming *prima ballerina* is your tail. But you will succeed, my dear. Of this I am certain. In the meantime, we are fortunate that our next ballet is *The Nutcracker.* The role of Clara is perfect for you."

The role of Clara was perfect because Clara was a child.

Madame Giselle had chosen twenty young

students from the ballet school to play children in the first act of *The Nutcracker*. These little mice would all wear training ribbons. And, as Madame Giselle had pointed out, it would be awkward if Clara, who was also supposed to be a child, did not also wear a ribbon. According to the ballet mistress, *The Nutcracker* would be the perfect opportunity to showcase Esmeralda's talents. "You can wear the training ribbon, and nobody will care," Madame Giselle had observed.

The ballet mistress had adjusted Clara's choreography so that the dances Esmeralda would perform would be much more difficult than those performed by the student dancer who would play Clara in the human ballet. The dances were so difficult, in fact, that Esmeralda felt compelled to practice them day and night. She practiced them at rehearsals with the other dancers, and she practiced them when she was alone.

Only a few days ago, she had been practicing in

the costume department. Late in the day, Esmeralda had been working on her *piqué* turns, spinning across the floor beneath one of the cupboards. She had lost herself in the moment, imagining herself whirling across the stage on opening night, and she had danced right out from under the cupboard, coming to rest in a perfect *arabesque,* her arms outstretched and her body turned slightly toward an imaginary audience.

Except that the audience hadn't been imaginary. Much to Esmeralda's horror, a human girl had been watching her. The girl had stared at Esmeralda, her blue eyes wide with wonder.

The girl had stared . . . and smiled. And then a voice had called out, "Irina! Irinushka! Where are you?"

"I'm here, Papa!" the girl had answered, breaking the spell. Esmeralda had run back under the cupboard, and the girl—Irina—had run out of the room.

But Esmeralda still thought about Irina. From the girl's smile, Esmeralda had been able to guess what she had been feeling: delight at seeing something wonderful. Thinking of Irina's smile gave Esmeralda hope that the mice of Saint Petersburg might feel that same delight.

The music on the other side of the wall stopped for a moment, then started again.

"Line up, everyone! We will practice our *piqué* turns," said Madame Giselle.

Eager to show what she could do, Esmeralda placed herself first in line. She made one, two, three, four turns down the narrow space between the walls before her tail broke free from the ribbon.

She heard a snickering from some of the dancers still in line, and then Madame Giselle's firm voice saying, "Try again, my dear!"

Esmeralda knew who had laughed. Fleur de Lys was standing in line with Franz; it was no surprise that these two mice—both of them known for their unpleasant personalities—were friends. Now, as Esmeralda walked past Fleur, she heard the *prima ballerina* murmur, "It never ceases to amaze me that someone who comes from one of the theater's great dancing families has to wear a training ribbon!"

Fleur did *not* come from one of the theater's great dancing families. She was an outsider who had petitioned to attend Madame Giselle's ballet school. She had superb technique and had advanced quickly because of it. Yet, for all her success, Fleur's dancing lacked the emotional quality that Madame Giselle praised in Conrad's dancing—and in Esmeralda's. "Never mind Fleur—she's jealous of you," Conrad was always telling Esmeralda. Whether that was true, Esmeralda couldn't say, but she couldn't help minding Fleur's spiteful comments. And, as she placed herself in line again and tied up her tail, she resolved to practice harder than ever—with the training ribbon and without.

CHAPTER 4

The Spice Cookie

IRINA HAD NOT TOLD anyone about the dancing mouse. Not her friends at school, who would have laughed at her. Not Mama, who would have scoffed and told her not to be silly. Not even Papa, who would only have pretended to believe her. But she *had* seen a mouse—a silvery-gray one— wearing a lavender-colored ribbon and dancing across the floor of the costume department. The mouse had performed a tiny *arabesque*. It had looked right at her! In that moment, Irina had somehow known it was a girl mouse.

Then, too, there were the mice she had seen watching *The Sleeping Beauty* from the tsar's box. She was sure they had been enjoying the dancing. She liked Papa's suggestion that the mice might have their own ballet company.

At home, Irina sometimes pretended that the bookshelf in her room was a stage and that her doll, Lyudmila, was a ballerina. Where, she wondered, did the mice hold *their* performances? Did they have a mouse-size stage under the big stage? Once, during a rehearsal, Papa had shown Irina what it was like down there. It was dark, with only a small amount of light coming from the orchestra pit. Moreover, the noise of toe shoes striking the floor of the stage above was loud and distracting. That the mice should have to perform in such conditions bothered Irina.

One night in late October, the boiler in the furnace room at Irina's school burst. The students were to have an unexpected vacation while it was being repaired, and Papa and Mama, unable to leave Irina at home alone, had to bring her to the theater with them.

On Irina's first morning at the theater, she helped Mama sew hems on the party dresses that would be worn by the children in the first act of *The Nutcracker*. Mama's supervisor, Madame Federova, rewarded Irina by giving her some scraps of cloth and ribbon to use for making doll dresses. The greater reward came near the end of the day, when Papa asked if Irina would like to watch the students from the ballet school rehearse on stage.

Now Irina settled herself into one of the theater seats. She glanced up at the tsar's box. No mice today. Then, from the pocket of her pinafore, she pulled out Lyudmila. Papa had carved the tiny doll from bits of wood, painting a serene, artistic expression on her face, and fitting her together in such a way that her arms and legs could bend. Irina

set Lyudmila on the arm of the theater seat so that she could see the stage.

The assistant ballet master, Monsieur Ivanov, was sitting a few rows in front of her. His head turned back and forth as he watched the students dancing to the lively music being played by the rehearsal pianist. Irina kept her eyes on the girl dancing the role of Clara. Even now, Mama was upstairs working on Clara's costume. It would be white with ruffles and a sash of crimson satin. Irina was already planning to make a similar dress for Lyudmila.

Suddenly, Monsieur Ivanov leaped to his feet. "No, no, no!" he shouted, and the music came to a halt.

The assistant ballet master strode down the aisle and up onto the stage. "Now then, children! You must form two circles when you dance: two *precise* circles, one inside the other. When the music changes, you must open up, regroup, and form a figure eight. As for you, Clara—what's your name again?"

The student bobbed in a curtsy. "Stanislava, Monsieur Ivanov."

"I am aware that you are talented, Stanislava, but I don't want you outshining the other dancers. It's too much of a distraction. Three simple *châiné* turns are all that is required; no *piqué* turns!"

Irina didn't agree. Stanislava was clearly capable of performing the *piqué* turns. Just think how lovely they would look when she was wearing her ruffled costume!

"Yes, Monsieur. I am sorry. I will do it right this time," said Stanislava.

The music started up again. The children danced. Monsieur Ivanov returned to his seat. "Remember to smile, Clara!" he shouted above the piano.

Yes, thought Irina, this *was* supposed to be a happy scene. Later on, however, Clara would *not* be smiling. Not when dancers dressed as mice invaded the stage. Then Clara would have to look frightened.

Irina thought of the real mice, trying to perform

The Nutcracker on their tiny stage. Wouldn't it be silly for the mouse Clara to be afraid of mice?

Just then she felt something tickle her neck. Startled, she looked up to see Papa holding a feather duster. He used it to point toward the rear of the theater.

She slipped Lyudmila into her pocket and followed him out to the lobby.

"It's time to go home, Irina. Will you go fetch Mama from the costume department?"

"Yes, Papa."

"And listen—I've got a treat for you. Today was Yuri Petrovich's birthday—you remember him, don't you?"

She nodded. Yuri Petrovich was one of the custodians—the nicest custodian after Papa.

"His wife baked cookies, and he brought some to work for us to enjoy. I saved one for you."

It was a spice cookie, smelling of honey and nutmeg and anise, and covered with snowy-white icing. Irina's mouth watered as she took it from Papa. "May I eat it now?"

He laughed. "I think you'd better before I decide to eat it myself. Hurry, now! Go tell Mama that I'll meet both of you in the cloakroom."

Irina headed upstairs. But she didn't eat the spice cookie.

Not because she wasn't hungry, nor because she didn't love spice cookies. Rather, because it occurred to her that she knew someone else who might like them too.

CHAPTER 5

Konstantin Grigorovich Gurkin

ALMOST AS SOON AS a mousetrap at the Mariinsky was baited, somebody was sure to steal the food. Nevertheless, Esmeralda always held out hope that she might find something to eat in the mousetrap under the cupboard in the costume department. The trap was an easy stop on her way home from rehearsal, so she always checked it.

One evening she arrived later than usual, rehearsal for *The Nutcracker* having dragged on after hours.

Monsieur Ivanov had been working with the students from the ballet school, making sure *they* knew the choreography for the children's dances in the first act. Correspondingly, Madame Giselle had worked all afternoon with Esmeralda and the children from the mouse ballet school, making sure *they* knew the choreography. Esmeralda's tail had popped free of the training ribbon several times, and she was worn out and disappointed by her performance. Worse, her day was not over, for tonight she was scheduled to go out on her first scrounge patrol. If she didn't hurry, she would be late.

Oh, but she was hungry! Would there be something to eat in the trap?

No! Once again, another mouse had come before her—a careless mouse who had forgotten to retrieve the kopek. The mouse had left the coin in plain sight, where a human could find it easily. Just suppose the custodians were to figure out how the mice were springing the traps! Just suppose they decided to set new traps that were even harder to outsmart than these!

Sighing, Esmeralda picked up the kopek. She found a crack in the floorboards nearby and nestled the coin inside, where she knew she could find it the next time she checked the mousetrap.

As she turned to head home, however, she saw something on the floor not far away. She went over to investigate, but she smelled what it was even before she reached the big, round cookie. Esmeralda breathed in an aroma of nutmeg and honey and anise. She nibbled at the icing and closed her eyes with pleasure.

A whole cookie! Somebody must have dropped it. What a lucky day!

But it was so big. Could she carry it to the attic? Maybe she could try rolling it, or —

Just then, Esmeralda heard a noise. She darted into the shadows.

A moment later a man peered under the

cupboard. Esmeralda recognized him and edged back farther into the darkness. Konstantin Grigorovich Gurkin was the first assistant custodian at the theater. None of the mice liked him. Gurkin was always calling them *vermin,* an ugly word that his supervisor, chief custodian Mikhail Danilovich Chernov, never used.

Gurkin's searching gaze alighted on the mousetrap. Seeing that it was sprung, he gave a dissatisfied grunt. He poked a broom under the cupboard, sweeping its bristles in an arc that barely missed Esmeralda but pulled the trap — and the cookie and a great quantity of dust — out from under the cupboard.

"Waste of lard," the custodian muttered as he baited the mousetrap. "Waste of time setting traps in the first place, when people are so careless with food. Why not just invite the vermin to tea?"

Gurkin slid the trap back under the cupboard. He swept up the dust and the spice cookie. Esmeralda

heard a clatter as he emptied his dustpan into the wastebasket.

Only when the custodian had clumped out of the room did she dare retrieve the kopek. She tossed it at the trap. *Snap!* She put the coin back in its hiding place and scooped up the lard. It wasn't nearly as appetizing as the lost treat, but it *was* food and she *was* hungry. Her brother and Conrad would be hungry, too. She wouldn't even tell them about the cookie, Esmeralda decided as she hurried off to the attic.

CHAPTER 6

Maksim

GRINGOIRE NOT ONLY loved to read, but he also loved to write. He dabbled in poetry and had aspirations of becoming a playwright. He also kept a diary, using a pencil that had been sharpened to a stub to record his experiences on cigarette papers stolen from the theater director's office.

He was working on his diary when Esmeralda reached the attic. He looked up and said, "Ah, there you are. Conrad's already come and gone."

"Gone!"

"He said not to worry; he'll take your place on scrounge patrol."

"Oh, no!" Esmeralda thrust the sticky lard at her brother and ran back the way she had come. It wasn't right for Conrad to take on her responsibility. He must be as tired as she was!

She made her way down to the rendezvous point — a crack in the stonework at the back of the theater — and squeezed through. The air was chilly and the moon already up. There were no mice to be seen, but Esmeralda recalled Conrad mentioning that they usually scrounged for food behind a bakery near the theater. Her parents had taken her to the bakery when she was small, and she was certain she still knew the way. She must follow the path along the canal behind the Mariinsky. She must cross the first bridge she came to, and the bakery would be in sight on the other side of the water.

Alas! Halfway across the bridge, Esmeralda could see that she was wrong. The bakery she remembered was gone. A sign in the window indicated that the shop now sold carpets. Her cousin and the scrounge patrol were nowhere to be seen.

A cart rolled toward her. She leaped out of its path and nearly tumbled into the canal. She backed away from the parapet, turned, and found herself face-to-face with two rats.

Their fur was slick and smelled of fish. "What have we got here?" said the larger rat.

"A wee little mouse," said the smaller rat—who wasn't *much* smaller.

"Very little. She looks hungry."

"Maybe we should drop her in the river so she can go fishing."

"Please let me by!" said Esmeralda.

"Listen to her—very polite, isn't she?" said the larger rat.

The smaller rat sneered. "I'm surprised she can speak Russian. Those Mariinsky mice always speak French. All hoity-toity."

"I'm as Russian as you are!" Esmeralda's temper was up now.

"Let's not drop her in the river," said the larger rat. "I'm hungrier than she is. Not much meat on her bones, but there might be enough for a snack later on."

He must be bluffing. Rats didn't eat mice. At least, Esmeralda didn't think they did.

The larger rat stepped toward her. Esmeralda picked up a pebble. She lifted it above her head, ready to throw it. "Let me pass!" she said.

The larger rat guffawed. The smaller rat snickered.

Suddenly, a mouse pushed his way between the rats. He strode over to Esmeralda, turned, and faced her tormentors. His shadow stretched out impressively as he said, "You heard the lady."

"Maksim!" said the larger rat. The smaller rat shrank back.

The mouse nodded. "That's right. Now, get off

my bridge before I call for some reinforcements."

To Esmeralda's astonishment, the rats did just that. Silently, they waddled away, rounded the end of the bridge, and slid off the embankment into the canal.

Esmeralda dropped the pebble. She stared at the mouse. He appeared tough and sturdy, with charcoal-colored fur and a piratical-looking scar just below his eye. If he hadn't just helped her, she might have felt wary of him. She said, "Thank you! Is this really your bridge?"

The mouse grinned. "Well, I have an agreement with a cat that lives under it. I bring him things—treats, you know—and he offers some protection in return. Those rats know better than to act the way they did. They're a pair of bullies. This is their idea of fun."

"I don't like rats," said Esmeralda, though, in truth, she had never met any before tonight.

"They're not all like that. Some of my best friends are rats."

A mouse who was friends with rats? Esmeralda had never heard of such a thing.

He must have guessed what she was thinking. "I'm friends with just about everybody," he explained. "There's hardly a mouse or a rat or a dog or a cat in Saint Petersburg who doesn't know Maksim!"

"You haven't seen other mice tonight, have you?" asked Esmeralda. "A group from the Mariinsky?"

"You're from the theater, eh? No, I haven't seen anybody tonight. My guess is your friends are at the bakery. That's where they always go. Not that there's ever much to find there."

"But the bakery is closed." Esmeralda pointed across the bridge.

Maksim shook his head. "There's a new bakery. It isn't far. I can take you there, if you like."

Conrad would want her to go back home,

Esmeralda knew. He was always telling her how dangerous Saint Petersburg was — always warning her to beware of strangers.

Certainly, Maksim was a stranger. But she liked him already, and he was completely at ease talking to rats — and even cats. Esmeralda said, "Thank you! I'd like that very much."

He led her back the way she had come. They walked side by side along the stone path. As they passed the mouse entrance to the theater, Maksim commented, "No show tonight."

"No, not tonight."

"I suppose you must be a dancer if you're from the Mariinsky."

"Yes, though I've only just joined the company. I haven't danced in any of the productions yet."

"In the company! Say, you're talking to a real fan. My friends and I go to the ballet whenever we can."

Esmeralda's interest was piqued. She had never

met an actual balletomane before. "Did you see *The Sleeping Beauty*?" she asked.

"Ah, *The Sleeping Beauty*! Very romantic!"

"My cousin was in it. He played Prince Désiré."

Maksim stopped for a moment. "I'm sorry . . ." He looked at her questioningly; she could tell he wanted to know her name.

"Esmeralda."

"Right, Esmeralda. My friends saw your cousin, but I'm afraid I haven't seen a mouse production in some time."

Esmeralda tried to hide her disappointment. She shouldn't be surprised that Maksim preferred the human productions. Was it the dancing that he liked better, or the costumes and sets—the *spectacle,* as Madame Giselle called it?

Before she could ask him, Maksim touched her arm. He pointed and said, "There's the bakery, and there's the rubbish bin. No sign of your friends."

The narrow alleyway was quiet and lonely. Esmeralda said, "But I'm sure Conrad said they were going to the bakery."

Maksim looked thoughtful. "It doesn't look like this bakery owner has even put out the garbage. Maybe your friends tried their luck at some other place. Where else do they like to go?"

"I don't know. I've never gone out with them before." Esmeralda couldn't mask her disappointment. "I suppose I should just go home."

"You could. But . . . if I can make an observation, Esmeralda?"

"Yes?"

"You look a little hungry."

"I am, rather . . ." Esmeralda thought of the lost spice cookie.

"I'd like to take you out to eat."

The way Maksim said those words—as if it would be a pleasure to him if she said *yes,* and a disappointment if she said *no*—made Esmeralda's heart skip a beat. It occurred to her that Maksim was a rather handsome-looking pirate.

Still, she hesitated. What if Conrad came home before she did? He and Gringoire would wonder what had happened to her.

On the other hand, if she did go with Maksim, she could ask him more questions about the human ballets he had seen. Perhaps she would find out something that could help the Russian Mouse Ballet Company.

It was a perfectly good reason for saying *yes*, and Esmeralda seized upon it. "All right," she said.

Maksim's smile widened. He said, "Come on, then! We'll go to Nevsky Prospect!"

CHAPTER 7

Nevsky Prospect

ESMERALDA HAD NEVER BEEN to Saint Petersburg's main thoroughfare. She had only heard about Nevsky Prospect and its fancy shops and restaurants. "Is it far?" she asked.

"We'll hitch a ride. We'll be there in no time at all," said Maksim.

Hitch a ride . . . What did that mean? Maksim had already brought Esmeralda back to the little bridge. They had not crossed it but instead had turned onto a new street, bustling with horses, carts, carriages, and people. Maksim didn't seem to care if anybody saw them. He took Esmeralda's hand and hurried toward a carriage stopped at the side of the road to let in some human passengers. "This will do!" he said.

The coachman atop the carriage cracked his whip. The horses stirred and strained, and the carriage started to move. "Up we go!" shouted Maksim, and he grabbed hold of a spoke on one of the wheels. He was lifted up into the air as the cart rolled forward. Maksim reached down and pulled Esmeralda up beside him. "Grab hold!"

Esmeralda wrapped her arms around the spoke. The wheel turned and she squeezed her eyes shut. She was sideways. She was upside down. She was going to be sick!

Maksim said, "Move around to the other side of the wheel."

She turned herself around on the spoke so that

she was facing out. She opened her eyes, caught a glimpse of upside-down buildings in the distance, then quickly closed her eyes again.

"Less easy for someone to spot us here," Maksim shouted above the noise of the traffic. "If you look over there . . ." He waited for her to open her eyes. He let go with one hand and gestured in a careless way that made Esmeralda worry he might go flying off the rotating wheel. "Over there, you might catch a glimpse of the Moyka River. And you might think it's the Neva River. A lot of mice make that mistake. But let me tell you, the Neva is much bigger! And beyond the Moyka, a few streets away, is the Alexander Garden. Very romantic in summer!"

Romance was the last thing on Esmeralda's mind. "Are we almost there?" she gasped.

"To the Alexander Garden? No. To Nevsky Prospect? Yes, nearly. We're lucky there's so little traffic at this hour—and such a speedy carriage! I saw a coat of arms on the door. I think it's somebody important—a count or a baron or even a prince. Who knows? Everybody who's anybody goes to Nevsky Prospect!"

Round and round and round they went, until Maksim shouted, "When I give the word, jump and roll away from the carriage."

There was no time to think. "Now!" Maksim told Esmeralda.

She jumped, hit the ground, and rolled.

Maksim pulled her out of the way of another carriage. "Watch out so you don't get crushed!" He steered her around some men who were shouting at each other.

A dog barked and Esmeralda froze. Maksim said, "Don't worry! He's far away." He led her across a cobbled walk and into a narrow space between two buildings. He gestured toward the street. "Take a look!"

Esmeralda stared. She was sure even the Neva River couldn't be wider than the street in front of her. On one side of it, the horse-drawn carriages went one way; on the other side, they traveled in the opposite direction. And in the middle of the street, horses pulled double-decker trolley cars filled with people. Still more people were strolling along and across the street, creating patterns like dancers on a stage.

"What do you think?" asked Maksim.

Snow—the first of the season—had begun to fall. Star-like crystals shimmered in the light from the streetlamps, and Esmeralda thought of the "Waltz of the Snowflakes" in *The Nutcracker.* She thought of Monsieur Petipa. No wonder he worked so hard to turn his ballets into *spectacles.* How else could he hope to lure the people of Saint Petersburg away from the magnificent show that was Nevsky Prospect? And no wonder a mouse like Maksim, familiar with such grandeur, would prefer Monsieur Petipa's productions!

She said, "It's amazing!"

"I knew you'd like it!" said Maksim. "See that building over there?"

Esmeralda looked up at an elegant four-story stone structure. Its first floor was dark, but its tall second-story windows blazed with light.

"There's a restaurant upstairs—very fancy," said Maksim. "Even Tchaikovsky likes to eat there. Just wait until you see what they throw out in the trash behind the building!"

The restaurant's garbage bins were overflowing with cabbage leaves, loaves of bread, carrot peelings, apple cores, half-eaten pastries, and more. Esmeralda gazed, openmouthed. "I never saw so much food!"

They weren't alone. Maksim tossed out a greeting to a pair of rats hovering over a meaty-looking bone: "Hello, Modest . . . Pyotr! Mind if we look around?"

The rats nodded a greeting.

Maksim said, "Look! Here's half a pancake for us."

"What's that black stuff on it?"

"Caviar. Whoops—careful! I think it's spoiled. Try this." Maksim pushed a slightly less fragrant bread roll toward Esmeralda. It was filled with some kind of stuffing.

She nibbled, tasting flavors new to her tongue. She said, "I wish I could take this home."

"Maybe not that *pirozhok*. But there might be some cake—"

Esmeralda gave a cry. "Look! A whole potato!" She had a vision of herself carrying the potato into the Mariinsky. She would be a hero if she could bring home that much food!

And if she could bring home some ideas for attracting audiences to *The Nutcracker*. She mustn't forget her other reason for coming here with Maksim.

Esmeralda was about to ask him what he had thought of *The Sleeping Beauty* when she paused, sniffing the air.

What smell was that? Sugary and sweet. Maybe a little *too* sweet.

She spotted the source of the smell: a ball as big as a ripe cherry, but with pink and white stripes. She had seen something like it in the set design for the second act of *The Nutcracker*. "Is it a sugar plum?" she wondered aloud. Gringoire had explained that a sugar plum was a kind of candy.

She moved in for a closer look, and the smell hit her like a slap. Her legs grew weak and she fell forward.

She turned to look for Maksim. The movement made her feel as if her head had spun off her neck. She looked back at the . . . whatever it was . . . sugar something . . . She couldn't remember. Her head ached too much.

"Maksim?" Esmeralda called as the smell enveloped her.

But she didn't know whether he heard her, because the world went black.

CHAPTER 8

The Balalaika Café

I THINK SHE'S WAKING UP!"

Esmeralda opened her eyes.

A rat was staring at her. Not one rat, but two . . . and a concerned-looking mouse with a piratical scar under his eye. *Maksim.*

Esmeralda sat up and swayed. Her head ached, but the sickening smell was gone.

Maksim put his arm around her. "How do you feel?"

"A bit queasy." She looked around. She was in a dark room, lit only by the moonlight from a window high above her. The air was warm. She could hear the faint sound of music.

"What happened? Where am I?"

"You fainted! This is a bookstore."

Sure enough, Esmeralda could smell books. Now she noticed them, standing up cover to cover on shelves, the gold-embossed titles on their spines glistening in the light from the window. And the shelves were so high! They rose up like buildings, disappearing into the darkness above. How could there be so many books?

"Pyotr and Modest helped me bring you inside," said Maksim.

The two rats looked exactly alike, with scruffy brown fur and blunt noses. Esmeralda guessed they must be brothers. She said, "Thank you."

"No trouble," said one of them.

"No trouble at all," said the other.

Esmeralda said, "I've never fainted before."

Maksim's smile made his eyes crinkle up at

the corners. "You've probably never met up with a peppermint before."

"A pepper . . . mint?"

"It's a type of candy. Humans love them, but mice hate peppermints. They're not poisonous, but the smell of peppermint oil can make you feel sick. It made *you* feel so sick you passed out!" said Maksim. "I live in a house where they use peppermint oil to keep us away from the food. The people smear it on the boards at the front of the cupboards. Peppermint oil is dreadful stuff, but easy enough to avoid if you recognize the smell."

Just thinking of the smell made Esmeralda's stomach give a flop. "How long have I been . . ." She searched for the right word.

"Unconscious?" Maksim finished. "Not so very long. Are you still hungry?"

In spite of the queasy feeling, she was. Esmeralda nodded.

"Good. We'll take you to the Balalaika Café."

"The what?"

"You'll see."

Maksim held out his hand. Esmeralda hesitated, feeling suddenly shy. But she let him help her up. She said, "We're not going to ride on a carriage wheel again, are we?"

Maksim laughed. "No carriage wheel needed," he promised.

They didn't go outside. Instead, Maksim led Esmeralda past row after row of towering bookshelves, with Modest and Pyotr following behind. The music Esmeralda had noticed before grew louder.

At last, Maksim led her around a bookshelf and said, "Welcome to the Balalaika Café!"

To Esmeralda's astonishment, the floor in front of her was crowded with mice. They sat and stood in groups, eating and laughing and talking above the music. Here and there she saw a few rats as well.

"It isn't really a café," said Maksim. "It's just a place we all like to come. The music comes from the restaurant upstairs. A balalaika orchestra plays there almost every night."

"And the food?" Esmeralda wondered aloud.

"We get it from that garbage heap outside the building. Generally, we're expected to bring something to share. But don't worry, my friends won't mind that we're empty-handed."

Three mice sitting in the middle of the crowd were waving to Maksim. He waved back, even as other mice shouted *hello* to him. Modest and Pyotr seemed to be almost as popular, and they were already making their way toward a group of rats sitting below a window. "Come on," said Maksim. "I'll introduce you."

As they crossed the floor, Esmeralda found herself being introduced again and again. Everyone in the café seemed to consider Maksim a close friend. At last, they reached the three mice who had waved, and Esmeralda learned that their names were Dmitri, Igor, and Nadya. The first two were brothers, close in age to Maksim. "We grew up together," Maksim explained.

As for Nadya, she was Igor and Dmitri's aunt, and everyone, including Maksim, called her Auntie Nadya. When Maksim introduced Esmeralda as a dancer in the Russian Mouse Ballet Company, Nadya drew Esmeralda over to sit with her. "A ballerina from the Mariinsky! But I don't recognize you . . ."

"I'm new to the *corps de ballet*," Esmeralda explained. "But I do have a part in our next production—a new ballet with music by Tchaikovsky."

"We love Tchaikovsky!" said Nadya. "The music for *The Sleeping Beauty* was beautiful."

The music for *The Nutcracker* would be beautiful as well, thought Esmeralda. But what about everything else? Without sets and costumes, the mouse production might seem drab to these sophisticated balletomanes.

"But tell me — how do you know our dear Maksim?" said Nadya.

"He rescued me from some rats," said Esmeralda.

"Nonsense!" said Maksim. "You were handling those bullies very well before I came along. It was the peppermint that nearly did you in."

Maksim told everyone what had happened. He added, "I think Esmeralda will feel better if she eats something."

Nadya said, "You poor thing! You must be starving! We have plenty of food. Do you like cheese?"

Esmeralda couldn't remember her last meal that wasn't lard and bread. She took the piece of cheese Dmitri broke off for her and thanked him.

Between bites, she asked Nadya questions: Had

she seen both productions of *The Sleeping Beauty*? And what had she thought of them — particularly the mouse production?

"Oh, yes, Dmitri and Igor and I saw both productions. Such a beautiful story — so romantic. The human production was splendid! The costumes were so colorful. And the sets — I really felt as if I were looking at a real castle!"

"The mouse production didn't have costumes or sets. I suppose that must have been . . . disappointing?" Esmeralda's voice rose in a question.

Igor spoke up then. "*Disappointing* isn't exactly the word I'd use. Why, Dmitri fell asleep in the second act —"

"I did not!" Dmitri protested.

Igor shrugged. "All right. Maybe I was the one who fell asleep!"

"Please forgive my nephew, Esmeralda," said Nadya. "We liked the mouse production very much."

Dmitri added, "It was . . . well, different from the human production."

Different, and not in a good way, thought Esmeralda. For all that Nadya and Dmitri were trying to be kind, she could tell they hadn't liked the mouse production as much as the human one.

Nadya said, "Prince Désiré was outstanding."

"That was Conrad. He's my cousin."

Nadya brightened. "Such a fine dancer—and so handsome! If I'm not mistaken, he is related to the great Medora."

"She was our grandmother," said Esmeralda.

"Conrad's the best dancer in the company," Dmitri declared.

"Not like that other one—what's her name?—Fleur de Lys," said Igor. He was shorter and stouter than his brother. He also smiled less often.

"She has good technique!" argued Dmitri.

"But the feeling! The emotion! Where is it? I tell you, the Russian Mouse Ballet Company isn't what it used to be. You've said it yourself, Auntie!" said his brother.

Nadya frowned at Igor. So did Dmitri and Maksim.

"You're too critical, Nephew," Nadya chided. She turned to Esmeralda. "We can't wait to see *you* dance at the Mariinsky, my dear."

"Speaking of *dancing*," said Maksim, nodding toward something behind Nadya.

Esmeralda turned and saw that the crowd of mice was moving back, leaving a large space on the floor. Nadya gently pulled Esmeralda back as well. "Time for some fun!" she said.

Music often made Esmeralda think of a conversation. One instrument or instruments would say something, and another instrument or instruments would respond. Sometimes the instruments would talk over and around one another until coming into agreement at the end of a song. And sometimes—and this was one of the reasons Esmeralda loved to dance—the instruments seemed to tell a story.

The balalaikas being plucked and strummed by the musicians in the orchestra upstairs were cheery conversationalists. They had been getting along well all evening, like friends telling one another amusing tales. Now, as they began a new tune, they seemed to become aware that they had other listeners. "So, you've noticed us!" the balalaikas seemed to say. "Well, then, pay attention!"

A murmur of approval ran through the café. "I love this song!" Maksim exclaimed.

Esmeralda liked it, too. Just now, the tune was slow. And yet, there was something in the music that said, "Just you wait!" Indeed, the dancers were not waiting. They crowded onto the floor, forming couples and bowing to each other as the balalaikas played a succession of stately chords. Nadya said, "You and Maksim should dance, Esmeralda."

"Oh, no!" said Esmeralda. "I mean—I don't feel quite well enough. But Maksim should dance." She could tell that the music was tugging at him. She knew exactly how that felt.

Nadya said, "Igor! Dmitri! Get up and dance with Maksim. Esmeralda and I will watch and enjoy."

Maksim allowed Igor and Dmitri to pull him onto the floor. The balalaikas seemed to have been waiting for them, for the music slowed—the notes hanging in the air as the three friends took their places. And then, suddenly, with the clash of a tambourine, the music took off like a rabbit sprinting across a meadow.

Faster and faster the balalaikas played. Faster and faster, until the dancers struggled to keep up. More and more dropped out until there were only three mice on the floor. The crowd cheered as Maksim, Dmitri, and Igor leaped and cavorted. First Maksim

jumped into the air, turning one and a half times around before landing. Then Igor, and then Dmitri, and then Maksim again. The dance was a contest in which the friends tried to outperform one another with daring, acrobatic feats. Then, suddenly, each mouse dropped to a crouch, raised his arms, and began to kick his legs in time to the music.

Esmeralda looked around. The audience was having as much fun as the dancers — clapping and cheering and laughing. And now Maksim, Igor, and Dmitri were standing and spinning in unison. Their tails spun around them, forming hoops around their legs as the music grew louder still. Then, when it seemed impossible that they could continue, Dmitri leaped over Igor, Igor leaped over Maksim, and Maksim leaped over Dmitri, somersaulting in the air. He landed on one foot, just as the music came to a crashing conclusion.

The crowd roared its approval.

The three dancers fell to the floor, laughing and gasping for breath.

Nadya said, "What do you think?"

"I loved it!" Esmeralda exclaimed. "I've never seen anything so fast! We never dance like that at the Mariinsky!"

Nadya laughed. "I should think not!"

Maksim picked himself up and came over. He said, "Not exactly ballet, is it!"

"No!" said Esmeralda. "You were wonderful!" Almost as soon as she said these last words, she felt shy. Suppose Maksim should guess just *how* wonderful she thought he was!

If he did, he didn't let on. Maksim waved his hand dismissively. "Oh, it's just the way mice dance." Still, Esmeralda could tell he was pleased by her compliment.

His friends joined them. Dmitri said, "I'm sure you and your friends in the ballet company will show us a thing or two when we come to see *The Nutcracker*, Esmeralda!"

"I don't know about that!" Esmeralda thought about all the problems she had with her tail. She thought also of Igor's criticism of the Russian Mouse Ballet Company . . . asking where the feeling and emotion were. Why, the best dancers in the company didn't come anywhere close to showing the unbridled enthusiasm she had just witnessed here at the Balalaika Café. If the Saint Petersburg balletomanes were used to this type of dancing, how could the Russian Mouse Ballet Company hope to hold their interest?

Maksim misinterpreted her look of concern. He said, "Are you tired, Esmeralda?"

Nadya clucked her tongue. "Of course she is tired. From what I've heard, the dancers at the Mariinsky sleep at night so they can practice during the day. You must take her home, Maksim."

"I don't want to be a bother!" said Esmeralda.

"It's no bother," said Maksim. "If we leave now, I can get you back to the theater before dawn. And no carriage wheels this time. But you have to promise one thing, Esmeralda!"

"Yes?"

"The next time you come to the café, you must dance for us."

Maksim's smile made Esmeralda forget her worries about *The Nutcracker*. "I promise!" she said.

CHAPTER 9

The Missing Dress

OF ALL THE DANCES in *The Nutcracker*, the one Irina liked best was the solo variation that would be performed in the second act by the Sugar Plum Fairy. Monsieur Drigo, the Mariinsky's orchestra conductor, had let Irina play a few notes on the celesta, the keyboard instrument that would play the melody for the dance. The word *celesta*, Monsieur Drigo told her, came from the French word for "heavenly," but the delicate notes Irina played sounded more magical than heavenly. She could not help but think of the dancing mouse.

For more than a week now, Irina had been leaving food for the mouse. First, she had hidden Yuri Petrovich's spice cookie under the cupboard where she had seen the dancing mouse—the *mouse cupboard*, as she had come to think of it. The next morning, the cookie was gone. After that, Irina had left other food under the same cupboard—bread, mostly. The bread was always gone when she checked later.

Did that mean the dancing mouse was enjoying the treats? If only Irina could know for sure!

Then, one afternoon, something wonderful happened. Or rather, two wonderful things. And, quite possibly, a third.

The first wonderful thing was that Antonietta dell'Era, the Italian ballerina who would dance the role of the Sugar Plum Fairy, came to the costume department for a fitting, and Irina got to meet her in person.

Mama was in charge of making the Sugar Plum

Fairy costume. She pinned and repinned the bodice, and Mademoiselle dell'Era had to be patient and stand on a stool with her arms out to the side. "You are very good, Madame," the ballerina commented. "I cannot tell you how often seamstresses have stuck pins into me!"

"Thank you, Mademoiselle," said Mama.

They were speaking in French. The ballerina spoke with an Italian accent. Mademoiselle dell'Era asked, "Does your daughter speak French as well?"

"Yes, Mademoiselle. My mother was French, and my husband also speaks the language. Irina is fluent."

"Ah, yes? And let me guess: she wants to be a dancer when she grows up." Mademoiselle dell'Era smiled at Irina.

Mama laughed. "Well, she might dream of it. What little girl could not dream of such a life here at the Mariinsky? But to tell you the truth, I think she will be a dress designer."

When it came to her daughter's talent for sewing, Mama was unable to mask her pride. She said, "Irina, show Mademoiselle dell'Era the dress you have made for your doll!"

Irina reached into her pocket and brought out Lyudmila.

"Oh! See how tiny she is!" said Mademoiselle dell'Era. "May I hold her?"

Irina placed the doll in the ballerina's palm.

"Look at her dress! The lace! The beading! Did you really make this?"

"Yes, Mademoiselle!"

"She has made dozens of little dresses for her doll," said Mama.

"How does she do it?"

Irina took the dress off Lyudmila and described her method. "You cut a circle of cloth. You cut holes

for the head and the arms, stitch the hem, and sew on lace and beads." She put the dress back on Lyudmila. "You use a ribbon sash to gather up the cloth — like this."

"How clever! Your doll is a little ballerina, isn't she?"

"Yes, Mademoiselle," said Irina, adding, because it seemed the polite thing to say, and also because it was true, "but Lyudmila isn't a *prima ballerina* like you."

The second wonderful thing was that when the fitting was over, Mademoiselle dell'Era invited Irina to see her dressing room. "I am always receiving chocolates from my admirers. You may have one, if you like."

"May I go, Mama?"

"Yes, my dear." Feeling proud of her daughter always brought out Mama's indulgent side. "But hurry back and don't bother Mademoiselle dell'Era all afternoon."

Irina was so excited that she forgot to put Lyudmila back in her pocket. She only remembered her doll when she returned from the dressing room, having eaten not one but two chocolates and with two more wrapped up in a bit of paper for Mama and Papa.

"Where's Lyudmila?" she asked.

"You left her on the table. I laid her on top of my sewing basket."

The sewing basket was sitting on the floor, its lid shut tight. Lyudmila was not on top of the basket. Nor was she inside it. Irina said, "She's gone!"

Mama said, "She must have fallen. Get down and look on the floor."

Lyudmila was lying under the mouse cupboard. "Here she is — but her dress is gone!" Irina exclaimed.

"You took it off to show Mademoiselle dell'Era."

"I put it back on!"

"Then it must be here."

But the dress was missing. Mama said, "Never mind. You can put clothes on Lyudmila when you get home. After all, you have a box full of doll dresses."

"But someone has taken her dress!"

"Nonsense! Who would take it?"

And that was the third wonderful thing: Irina thought she knew.

CHAPTER 10

The Way Mice Dance

THE DRESS FIT PERFECTLY. Esmeralda tied the sash, then turned it so the bow was in the back, as it had been on the doll. She raised herself up on her toes and spun around, watching the skirt lift up like a cloud. Even in the dim light under the cupboard, the beads sparkled.

She stopped midturn. She had stolen a dress from a human girl—the very same girl who had caught her dancing before. Of course, it was wrong to steal, but Esmeralda couldn't allow herself to feel guilty. All she could think of was what Irina's mother had said: *You have a box full of doll dresses. . . .*

"A box full of doll dresses means a box full of costumes for *The Nutcracker*!" Esmeralda told Maksim that evening.

"Only if you can get them from that girl's house," he said.

They were at the Balalaika Café, sitting with Nadya, Igor, and Dmitri. It was Esmeralda's first time back since her initial visit, more than a week ago now. She hadn't expected to be back again so soon, but Maksim had shown up at the Mariinsky not two days after meeting Esmeralda, bringing savory treats for supper and regaling her brother and Conrad with colorful stories about his life in Saint Petersburg. At the end of the evening, Maksim had invited her to come dancing. "Some night when you're not on scrounge patrol," he had suggested.

Tonight was that night, and Esmeralda had already told Maksim how worried she was about *The Nutcracker* and the future of the Russian Mouse Ballet Company. Now she told everyone about a plan she had concocted. "Irina—she's the human girl I told you about, Maksim—is the daughter of the chief custodian. Irina doesn't come to the Mariinsky every day, but her father does, and he puts his coat in the cloakroom. I'll climb into the hem and—"

"What is a *hem*?" asked Dmitri.

"Well, it's like a tunnel at the bottom of a coat—just the right size for a mouse. I'll ride to Irina's house in the coat hem, wait until she goes to sleep, and gather up the dresses. I'll bring them back to the Mariinsky in the coat hem when her father comes to work the next morning."

"What if there's a dog or a cat?" asked Maksim.

Esmeralda frowned. She was proud of her plan, but she hadn't thought of dogs and cats.

Maksim said, "I think I'd better come with you."

"Oh, I couldn't ask you to —"

"I can help you. I'm good with dogs and cats."

Before she could say more, Igor spoke up. "It's going to take more than costumes to help *The Nutcracker*! They're saying mice are killed in the new ballet."

A prickle of alarm shot through Esmeralda. Was Franz spreading rumors, as Conrad had feared? She said quickly, "They aren't *really* killed."

"Of course they aren't!" Nadya's voice was soothing.

Igor went on. "You're supposed to believe they're killed, and you're supposed to feel happy about it, too. They say the mice in the ballet are villains. On top of all that, there's no romance in *The Nutcracker*." He took a bite of cheese. He chewed it vigorously, swallowed, and added, "The fact is, nobody wants to see this new ballet — not the human production or the mouse production. Costumes aren't going to change that!"

Igor tossed the last bit of cheese into his mouth. Only then did he notice that his aunt was glaring at him.

"Really, Igor!" said Nadya. "The things you say! *We* want to see *The Nutcracker*!"

Her nephew blinked in surprise. "I'm only saying what other mice are saying—"

"Hey!" Maksim said brightly. "This is a good song the orchestra's playing. How about we dance?"

Feeling numb, Esmeralda followed him onto the dance floor. All of Conrad's fears for *The Nutcracker* had come true: the city's most devoted balletomanes didn't want to see the new production. How foolish she was to think that costumes alone would solve the problem!

As it always did, the music chased away Esmeralda's worries. The tune was sprightly, and she was able to follow Maksim's lead without difficulty. She danced the way he did—not the way she did when she was at the Mariinsky, but the way all the mice danced here at the café—letting her tail move with her. She twirled three times to the left, then twirled three times to the right, and then clasped hands with Maksim, hopping from one foot to the other while crossing the floor. Maksim's tail whipped back and forth with each hop, and Esmeralda let hers do the same. All around them, couples were dancing together. It was, Esmeralda thought, just a little romantic.

The song ended. The crowd at the restaurant upstairs applauded. The mice on the floor waited to hear what the orchestra would play next.

When the next song began, the first chords rolled out slowly. The music was full of longing, as if the balalaikas were remembering a happier time.

Most of the dancers were leaving the floor. "Where is everyone going?" Esmeralda asked.

"Oh, they like fast music," said Maksim.

"I do, too. But this is beautiful!" said Esmeralda.

"I agree! Shall we dance?"

This time, Esmeralda led Maksim across the floor. She danced on her toes, adapting the choreography that would open the "Dance of the Sugar Plum Fairy" in the second act of *The Nutcracker*. Of course, when Fleur performed the same steps, she would keep her tail wrapped tightly around her body, but it seemed to Esmeralda that she must allow her tail to move with the music. Maksim let go of Esmeralda's hand and she danced away from him, swaying her upper body and letting the gentle motion travel down to the tip of her tail. She raised her arms and floated across the floor in a wide arc.

She heard a cheer—and more than a smattering of applause.

"They like your dancing," said Maksim, taking her hand again. He and Esmeralda danced together as the balalaikas ran up a scale and hovered on a note. Then, suddenly, the balalaikas ran down the scale. Esmeralda thought of a leaf falling from a tree. The balalaikas picked up a new tempo. The wind caught the leaf and tossed it up again. It was a fast song after all!

She let go of Maksim's hand and made one turn after another, snapping her tail to make herself spin faster than she ever had before.

The mice were clapping along with the music now. She was dancing alone. She could see Maksim watching her—clapping along with the crowd—with the *audience*. "You'll see," Conrad had once told Esmeralda. "When you're performing for an audience and they love your dancing, it's the most wonderful thing in the world. You'll feel just like you have a pair of wings."

Esmeralda's feet were her wings. They swept her across the floor, and she forgot about the audience. The music filled her up and propelled her forward. She leaped high, her tail flying out behind her. She ran and leaped again, this time turning twice in the air, something she had never been able to do when she wore the training ribbon at the Mariinsky.

The applause when the song ended nearly overwhelmed her. "More! More!" shouted the crowd.

Esmeralda wouldn't have thought she could give more. But the balalaikas began to play an exhilarating song that renewed her energy. Modest and Pyotr joined the dancing mice. The rats were strong. Modest lifted Esmeralda into the air. His brother stretched his arms out to the side, and Modest set Esmeralda on Pyotr's shoulder. The balalaikas slowed, creating a mood of suspense. Esmeralda balanced in an *arabesque* as Pyotr strode grandly around the floor. As the music grew even more quiet, she pulled her leg up into a *développé à la seconde.*

The crowd fell silent. Pyotr stood still. Esmeralda trembled from the effort of maintaining her pose. She held out one arm, and Modest reached up to

touch her hand. He steadied her, then let go, and she turned slowly around. A murmur of amazement passed through the crowd. Esmeralda felt a thrill that traveled all the way to the tip of her tail.

Suddenly, like a crash of thunder, the music picked up again. Esmeralda leaped from Pyotr's shoulder to Modest's arms. The rat set her down on the floor, and the crowd went wild as she performed one *fouetté* after another. Her tail snapped in the air and she could hear the mice counting the turns: *one, two, three, four* . . . She made it all the way to *thirty-two* before the music ended.

The crowd cheered and clapped.

Esmeralda knelt in a curtsy, just as she would have done at the Mariinsky.

Maksim ran over and embraced her. "They love your dancing!" he said. "They love *you!*"

CHAPTER 11

Mice Love Romance

THE NEXT MORNING, Esmeralda was late for class.

Very late. The rest of the company was already at floor practice when she arrived.

"I'm sorry, Madame Giselle. I didn't wake up on time."

The ballet mistress did not look pleased. "See that it doesn't happen again. Stretch at the barre now so you will be ready for rehearsal this afternoon."

"Yes, Madame."

Esmeralda had never been late to class before.

Nor would she be late again, she vowed as she began her workout.

All the same, she couldn't regret her night at the Balalaika Café.

Maksim had made sure she got back safely to the Mariinsky. They had walked partway—watching the moon glint on the Moyka River and talking. Esmeralda kept reliving the moment when Maksim had taken her hand in his.

When it had become too cold for walking and holding hands, they had ridden the rest of the way on the back of a carriage. Maksim had put his arm around her, protecting her from the cold, and they had kept right on talking.

Maksim was so easy to talk to.

"At the Mariinsky, we always dance *ballet*," Esmeralda had told him. "I love ballet, but it's so exciting to dance the way you do at the café. I loved making everyone happy when I danced."

"I know exactly what you mean," Maksim had

said. "When they cheer, you feel like you gave them a present. And I can tell you something else: don't believe all the things Igor was saying about *The Nutcracker*. If you dance like you did tonight, everyone will want to come see you, no matter what they've heard about the plot of the ballet."

Esmeralda wasn't sure of that. She didn't like talking about the problems she had with her tail. But somehow she hadn't minded telling Maksim. "It's different in ballet," she had explained. "You're supposed to keep your tail wrapped tightly around you. That's always been hard for me. Conrad says it's just a matter of technique. He says if I work hard enough, I won't even have to think about my tail anymore. But I've worked and worked, and I still have to wear a training ribbon."

"I never would have guessed you have such troubles, watching you dance tonight. When you did those fancy turns—so many of them—surely you were controlling your tail then!"

Esmeralda hadn't thought about it that way before.

"And those incredible leaps you made," Maksim had told her. "So high! You must have been controlling your tail then! The way you made it fly behind you! I tell you, Esmeralda, I have never seen any mouse dance the way you did tonight. I maintain that you *were* controlling your tail."

Perhaps Maksim was right, Esmeralda thought now. Last night, when she had danced, she had made her tail become a part of what she was doing. It wasn't as if she had forgotten about it; instead, she had controlled it in the same way she controlled her legs and her arms. If she set her mind to it, maybe she *could* learn to keep her tail in the proper ballet position, after all.

As it happened, Esmeralda had an unexpected break from dancing at rehearsal that afternoon. Due to a last-minute change in the human practice schedule, the mice would be rehearsing the beginning of the second act. Esmeralda had comparatively little dancing to do; she need only sit and pretend to enjoy the various entertainments put on for Clara in the Kingdom of Sweets.

Esmeralda watched the three soloists Madame Giselle had chosen to perform the Spanish dance. The music was lively; the dancers were good, though Esmeralda did wish they could be a little more *wild* in their movements.

Well, maybe not *quite* as wild as the dancers at the Balalaika Café. This was ballet, after all.

Still, the Spanish dancers could be a bit more enthusiastic. Costumes would help them *feel the music,* to borrow a phrase from Madame Giselle. Esmeralda wondered if Irina's box of doll clothes contained any brightly colored dresses. On her way home with Maksim, she had expressed doubts about stealing the dresses: what would be the point if mice weren't going to come see *The Nutcracker?*

But he had convinced her that the costume-stealing expedition would be worthwhile. "It seems to me that you won't forgive yourself if you don't at least try to save your ballet company," he had told her.

Then came the Arabian dancers. Soft colors would be good for their costumes, Esmeralda thought.

Her eyes focused on the bare wall behind the dancers, and she frowned. She knew what *should* be there—a set showing the marvelous Kingdom of Sweets. She had seen the design for it in Monsieur Vsevolozhsky's office—a painting full of colors. The human stage was sure to be breathtaking.

"Esmeralda!"

Above the music, Madame Giselle's voice was sharp.

"Please remember that Clara is supposed to be enjoying these entertainments," said the ballet mistress. "You might as well be *asleep* for all the enthusiasm you are showing. A moment ago you were frowning!"

The remark about falling asleep hit Esmeralda hard, for she thought of Igor falling asleep in *The Sleeping Beauty*. She said quickly, "I'm sorry, Madame!"

The Arabian dancers floated across the stage. Esmeralda tried to look entertained, adopting a pretend smile. She listened and thought how unfortunate it was that such beautiful, dreamy music was used to tell such a disappointing story. Igor was right when he said that mice loved romance. If only . . .

She listened to the music, letting her imagination go where it wanted, and an idea began to take shape in her mind.

It was an idea that might very well save *The Nutcracker*, and before long, Esmeralda's smile was real.

CHAPTER 12

A New Scenario

THAT EVENING, ESMERALDA told Conrad and Gringoire what she had learned from the balletomanes at the Balalaika Café. "I'm sure it's Franz who's spreading rumors," she said. "The Saint Petersburg mice have made up their minds that *The Nutcracker* is a terrible ballet. They don't want to watch the human production *or* the mouse production."

Conrad said, "Who can blame them? For once, the rumors are completely true! It *isn't* a good ballet."

"The music is good!"

"The story is awful."

"I know. The mice are villains, and there's no romance in it. But I've come up with a solution—actually, *you* came up with a solution," Esmeralda told Conrad. "You said it yourself: nothing short of a different ballet could save *The Nutcracker.*"

Her cousin looked at her blankly.

Esmeralda continued. "So, what if we turn *The Nutcracker* into a different ballet? What if we change the scenario and make it a romance?"

"A romance?" said Gringoire.

"I thought of it this afternoon during rehearsal. I was watching the Arabian dancers in the second act. I was listening to the music and I was picturing a different dance from the one I was seeing. I was picturing a romantic *pas de deux.*"

There was no need to reveal that she had pictured herself dancing with Maksim! Esmeralda hurried on. "The point is, as long as we match up our choreography to the music, we can tell any story we like!"

Gringoire looked skeptical. But Conrad was playing with his whiskers, something he tended to do when he was thinking. That was encouraging.

Esmeralda said, "Just think about the party scene in the first act. What if Clara Silberhaus isn't a child? What if she is a young lady? She could be dancing with someone she's in love with. . . ." Esmeralda could *hear* the music in her mind—she could *see* the scene: *Clara, dancing across the stage, only to fall into the arms of . . .*

"So the story wouldn't have to be completely different," Gringoire mused. "Just a few changes."

Esmeralda shook her head. "I think it should be *very* different. We need to give the Saint Petersburg mice everything they like to see in a ballet: romance and drama. And I think the mice should be heroes, not villains. I have all sorts of ideas; they only need to be written down."

She looked at her brother. It was a custom among the Mariinsky mice to name their children after characters in ballets. She was named after the captivating title character in *La Esmeralda*. Gringoire was named after a poet in the same ballet. Esmeralda had never felt herself to be particularly captivating, but there was no doubt in her mind that Gringoire had a poet inside him. "If anyone can rewrite the scenario for *The Nutcracker*, it's you," she told her brother. "You have such a way with words!"

Gringoire looked flattered, but unconvinced. "I may have a way with words, but I'm not so sure about ballets."

"We'll help you," Conrad said. "Esmeralda and I know the score by heart. We know what the music sounds like and can figure out what we might do differently from a dancing point of view."

Esmeralda nodded. "As I said, I think we can still have a party in the first act, only Clara Silberhaus won't be a girl, but a young lady."

"How about a young lady *mouse?*" said Conrad with a grin. "Clara Silber*haus*... Clara Silver*mouse!*"

Esmeralda laughed. "And Godfather Drossel-*mayer* can be—"

He finished her sentence. "Godfather Drossel-*mouse!*"

"Exactly! But rather than being Clara's godfather, I think he should be one of her many suitors. Only she won't like him very much. You know how the music is so sinister when he shows up. Well, what if he really *is* sinister, and she's repulsed by him?"

Conrad was nodding in agreement.

"Then what?" asked Gringoire.

Esmeralda already knew whose arms Clara must fall into. "I think the mouse king should also be at the party. Only he won't be bad in our version. He'll be good, and Clara will fall in love with him."

"There's your romance!" said Gringoire.

"What about the battle scene?" said Conrad.

"We'll still have it, because of the music," said

Esmeralda. "But in our ballet, it's the nutcracker who will be the villain."

Conrad said, "Would you kill him off in the battle?"

"Of course!" she said.

But Gringoire said, "I wonder—wouldn't it be more exciting if the mouse king was defeated in the battle and came back to rescue Clara in the second act? More suspenseful . . ."

Conrad clearly liked this idea. "Then we could have another battle!"

Esmeralda clapped her hands. "Yes! There's that wonderful music for the Russian *trepak*. The tambourine sounds just like clashing swords."

Her brother cleared his throat. "Am I supposed to be writing down this new scenario?"

"Oh, Gringoire. Would you, please?"

"I will. But I can't write as fast as you're talking. We may be up all night long."

• • •

They weren't up all night—not quite. It was nearly morning when Gringoire wrote the last line of the scenario.

"The audience will love it," said Conrad.

"They will indeed. Especially when they see our costumes and sets!" said Esmeralda, and she described her plan for obtaining the costumes.

Her cousin looked worried. "That sounds dangerous!"

"It's worth the risk, Conrad. You know it is!" said Esmeralda. "Besides, Maksim has offered to come with me." She hoped her brother and cousin wouldn't notice how excited she was by the prospect of what she was already thinking of as an adventure . . . and a romantic one at that.

But Gringoire merely said, "I think it's worth the risk. I, for one, would welcome a bit of pageantry on the stage. But you also mentioned *sets*, Esmeralda."

She nodded. "What about the set designer's sketches for *The Nutcracker*? I've seen them in the director's office. They're paintings on paper—just the right size for mice."

"How many paintings are there?" asked Conrad.

"Three," said Esmeralda. "There's the Silberhaus home and the pine forest in the first act, and the Kingdom of Sweets in the second act. Oh, Conrad, just think how beautiful the stage will look if we can have costumes and sets! The audience will love it."

"Madame Giselle won't."

"But the dancers will. Madame Giselle can't object when she sees how the costumes help everyone dance with more emotion."

Conrad was playing with his whiskers again. "I guess we'd have to steal the sets. But how would they fit through our tunnels?"

The Mariinsky mice used an elaborate system of passageways inside the walls and under the floors of the theater. They could gain access to every room by means of hidden entrances, but the tunnels and entrances would be too small for the paintings.

Gringoire said, "We can steal them at night—carry them through the halls when it's dark. As for getting them into our theater, I'm sure I can figure something out."

Conrad nodded, and then he yawned. "Speaking of *nights,* this one is nearly over. I'd like to get a few hours of sleep before morning."

When Esmeralda at last tumbled into bed, she lay in the dark and thought about how perfect the new ballet would be.

Costumes and sets and a romance! And not one but two thrilling battle scenes! The mice of Saint Petersburg would be lining up to see their production!

Conrad would play the mouse king, and she would dance the role of Clara, and . . .

It was only then that Esmeralda saw the flaw in her plan.

CHAPTER 13

For the Sake of the Company

*T*HE NEXT MORNING, Esmeralda and Conrad came to class early so they could share the new scenario with Madame Giselle. The ballet mistress paged through cigarette papers covered with Gringoire's handwriting, giving exclamations of pleasure as she went along:

"*Clara and the Mouse King!* A much better title than *The Nutcracker!*"

And, "Ah, yes! A romance is sure to please the audience."

And, "I love how you have worked the 'Waltz of the Snowflakes' into the story."

But as soon as she finished reading, she looked troubled. She said, "You do know what this means . . ."

Esmeralda nodded.

"What?" said Conrad. "What does it mean?"

Madame Giselle said, "How can Esmeralda dance the role of Clara?"

Esmeralda explained matters for her cousin. "In *Clara and the Mouse King*, Clara is a young lady mouse. She isn't a child, so she can't wear a training ribbon. Fleur will have to be Clara."

"But you deserve that role!" Conrad looked around to make sure nobody was listening, then added in a low voice, "Besides, you're a much better dancer than Fleur is!"

"Not if I can't keep my tail in position."

"But you can practice—"

"I've *been* practicing, and I know I'll get it

someday. But it's just too risky to hope that I'll master dancing without the training ribbon before the ballet opens. Just suppose I were to fail. Think of the reaction of the balletomanes in the audience!"

"Perhaps it is better that we not use this new scenario," said Madame Giselle.

Esmeralda shook her head. "If you heard what mice are saying about *The Nutcracker*, you wouldn't say that. Besides, there will be another ballet for me. There's more *likely* to be a new ballet if this one is a success. For the sake of the company, we have to stage *Clara and the Mouse King*."

Madame Giselle sighed. "I suppose you are right, my dear. It certainly is safer to have Fleur dance this role."

Conrad said, "But you *know* she's not as good as Esmeralda!"

Madame Giselle said, "Fleur does not bring as much emotion as Esmeralda does into her dancing, but her technique *is* flawless."

Costumes would help Fleur dance with more emotion, thought Esmeralda. So would sets. But she and Conrad had agreed not to tell Madame Giselle about their plans — not until they had the costumes and sets in hand.

The ballet mistress continued. "I hope you know that this decision is difficult for me, Esmeralda. I have said it before and I will say it again: you have the makings of a great ballerina."

Her words of praise brought a lump into Esmeralda's throat. "Thank you, Madame. I promise you, I'll work harder than ever. And I'm sure Fleur will be wonderful in *Clara and the Mouse King*."

Conrad was angry. "But what about Esmeralda, Madame Giselle? What role will she dance?"

The ballet mistress looked pained. "She will have to play one of the children."

That day at class, Esmeralda was determined to focus on her dancing. She tried to take comfort in

Madame Giselle's words of encouragement. She recalled what she had learned at the Balalaika Café. "I *can* control my tail," she reminded herself.

She tied on the training ribbon. She wasn't ready to dance without it, but today she would behave as if *she,* not the ribbon, were keeping her tail in the correct position.

She kept her mind focused, and her tail twitched only occasionally during practice at the barre. And, during floor practice, she managed to perform twelve *fouetté* turns—nothing like the thirty-two she had performed at the café, but a respectable number all the same. Unfortunately, her tail popped out of the ribbon on the thirteenth turn. Still, Esmeralda felt encouraged. She was sure she could have performed even more *fouettés* if she hadn't allowed herself to grow excited by success.

After class, as she was untying the training ribbon, Esmeralda overheard Fleur talking to Franz: "Madame Giselle told me all about the new

scenario. *Clara and the Mouse King*, it's to be called, and of course, Madame Giselle wants me to play Clara. After all, we can't have our *prima ballerina* wearing a training ribbon."

Franz glanced toward Esmeralda. Fleur looked around. Esmeralda couldn't tell whether her look of surprise was real or feigned.

Fleur said brightly, "Oh! There you are! You must be so relieved, Esmeralda."

"Relieved?"

"To still be playing one of the children in the ballet," said Fleur. "So you don't have to worry about your tail."

That hurt, and Esmeralda was pretty sure Fleur had meant it to hurt. "It's for the sake of the company," she told herself as she walked away. "There will be another ballet, and I will improve. And—"

Her next thought lifted her spirits.

And tonight she would see Maksim. Tonight they would get the costumes.

CHAPTER 14

Sliding Down a Rope

THAT EVENING IN THE cloakroom, in the woolly darkness of the hem of Mikhail Danilovich Chernov's coat, Esmeralda reviewed her plan for the night.

She had her supplies: a handkerchief and a coiled length of string. The handkerchief was one Conrad had found under a theater seat. It was embroidered with a pink letter *E*. Most likely, a lady named *Ekaterina* or *Elizaveta* had once owned it. "But I don't see why *E* can't stand for *Esmeralda*," Conrad had remarked. At any rate, Esmeralda liked to sleep under the handkerchief. And tonight, it would be perfect for carrying the costumes. As for the length of string, Esmeralda planned to secure one end to a coat button and the other end to the bundle of costumes, so that she could hoist them up into the coat hem.

She had everything she needed except her accomplice.

"Esmeralda?"

And here he was! She was relieved to hear Maksim's voice. She called, "I'm in a black coat. . . ." But there was more than one black coat. "There's a red scarf hanging on the same hook," she added.

"I see it! I'll be up straightaway!"

But he wasn't.

Esmeralda waited . . .

and waited . . .

She was about to poke her head out of the hem to look for Maksim when he said, "You *did* say a black coat with a scarf."

"Yes! A red scarf."

He gave a groan. "Oh, no! I've got the wrong coat. This scarf is green —"

At that moment, the cloakroom door opened. Maksim fell quiet and Esmeralda's heart lurched.

A voice said, "Ah, Mikhail Danilovich. You're leaving. But your wife and little girl are not with you."

Another voice, closer and somewhere above Esmeralda's hiding place, said, "My wife did her sewing at home today, so they are waiting for me there."

"Well, then. Good night to you!" said the first voice.

"Good night!" said Mikhail Danilovich.

Suddenly, Esmeralda was jerked up in the air. She was jostled up and down and sideways inside the coat hem. The custodian was indeed leaving, and it was too late for Maksim to join her inside the hem.

She felt the air change from warm to cold: Mikhail Danilovich must have left the theater. She could hear feet shuffling, wheels creaking, hooves clattering on pavement, and snatches of conversation. She could smell horses . . . and fish. Mikhail Danilovich must be walking along a canal or river.

A new noise assaulted her ears: a rhythmic *yap, yap, yap.* A dog!

"Down, you crazy mongrel! Down!" said Mikhail Danilovich.

Esmeralda felt herself bounced and jostled inside the hem as Irina's father began to jog. The dog's barking fell behind.

"You'd think I was carrying a pound of sausages in my coat!" muttered Mikhail Danilovich as he slowed to a walk.

Esmeralda's heart was pounding. What if the custodian had a dog waiting at home?

Or a cat?

Or a dog *and* a cat!

What a fool she was to have come up with this plan. Forget about getting the costumes. She would be lucky if she survived the night!

At last, Esmeralda heard a jingling of keys. She heard the sound of a door squeaking on its hinges and the stomping of boots. The coat shifted, and Esmeralda felt as if she were falling. A second later, she was swept upward and the coat stopped moving.

She heard a clatter of footsteps and a girl's voice. "Papa!"

"How's my Irinushka?"

"I'm good, Papa. Did you see Sasha outside? She went out earlier."

"I didn't see her."

Esmeralda wondered who Sasha was.

"Mama made dumplings for supper," said Irina. "Come in the kitchen to see!"

"I can smell the dumplings! Delicious!"

Esmeralda could smell them, too. She heard

Irina's mother say, "Put the plates on the table, Irina. How was work today, Misha?"

Mikhail Danilovich made a noise of despair. "Those mice will do me in!"

Mice! Esmeralda listened as Irina's father continued. "You already know how clever they are—how they've learned to set off the new mousetraps without getting caught. It seems that Gurkin fellow I told you about has informed the director that the traps were my idea."

"I thought it was Gurkin who suggested you buy them," said Irina's mother.

"So it was. But Gurkin is devious."

"Speaking of mice, did you know that Irina has been leaving food for them in the costume department? Madame Federova caught her at it yesterday. You should have heard your daughter, Misha! Telling Madame that the mice are hungry!"

"The mice *are* hungry!" said Irina. "And that Gurkin is mean, Papa!"

"Now then, you mustn't say such things," said Irina's mother.

Esmeralda remembered the cookie she had found under the cupboard in the costume department. She had found other things to eat there in recent days. She hadn't known Irina had left this food.

And here I've come to steal her doll dresses, thought Esmeralda with a pang of guilt. If only she could tell Irina how much the mice needed costumes. Surely, such a kindhearted girl would understand.

The Chernovs' supper was followed by a good deal of noise, which Esmeralda gathered was caused by something called *washing the dishes*. Afterward, Irina begged to be allowed to stay up and play with her doll. Her mother agreed, and apparently the family sat down close to the coat hem, for their voices were easy to hear.

Irina's mother said, "Hand me my sewing basket, please."

Irina chatted with her father. "I've made a new dress for Lyudmila, Papa."

"She looks very fine. I hope she won't be going to visit the tsar anytime soon."

"Why, Papa?"

"She'll outshine all the ladies at court; they won't allow that!"

Irina giggled. "Lyudmila belongs on the stage, not at court, Papa! Even Mademoiselle dell'Era says she's a dancer. This dress is a ballet costume!"

Esmeralda wondered what Irina would think if she knew that mice might soon be dancing in her doll's ballet costumes.

Presently, Irina's mother said, "It's time for bed."

"No, Mama!"

Irina's father said, "Do as Mama says, and I'll tell you a story."

Irina left the room and her father soon followed. Esmeralda strained to hear, trying to guess where they might have gone. Had Irina taken the doll—and the clothes—with her?

Some time passed before Irina's father returned. As he and Irina's mother readied themselves for bed, Esmeralda listened to their conversation.

"I'm more than a little worried about Gurkin," said Mikhail Danilovich. "He goes out of his way to curry favor with Monsieur Vsevolozhsky. Why, just the other day, the director asked me if I didn't think Gurkin deserved a promotion. What was I to say, when the only promotion available is my own job?"

His wife said, "I'm sure the director appreciates the hard work you do, my love! He would never think to replace you."

"I hope you're right," said Mikhail Danilovich with a sigh.

Irina's mother yawned. "I'm still not finished sewing this costume. I'll go in with you to the theater tomorrow. Irina doesn't have school, so she can come with us."

"Off to bed, then," said Mikhail Danilovich.

When the house was quiet, Esmeralda pushed the handkerchief out of the tiny hole she had made in the coat hem. She watched it fall to the floor, then put her arm through the coil of string and pushed her way out of the hole. She gripped the rough wool and crawled along the bottom of the coat. She climbed up the front until she found a wooden button. She looped one end of the string around the button several times, then let the rest of it snake down to the floor.

As far as thievery goes, there is nothing quite so thrilling—or satisfying—as sliding down a rope. Esmeralda slid down hers and looked around with something close to pleasure. She was standing on the edge of a carpet in a small sitting room. The windows let in enough light for her to see two chairs pulled up in front of a heating stove whose grate

still glowed red from the evening's fire. A sewing basket sat on the floor next to one of the chairs, its lid partially open. A bundle of tulle—the skirt of a ballet costume—tumbled out; Esmeralda could see the glint of a sewing needle stuck in the cloth.

The door leading outside was behind her; she could feel a cold draft flowing beneath it. Ahead of her, across the floor, were two other doors, both slightly ajar. Esmeralda would have to guess which one would lead her to Irina and the doll dresses. If only Maksim were here!

But he wasn't, she reminded herself. If the Russian Mouse Ballet Company was to have costumes, it was up to her to find them.

She gave the rope another tug. Still secure.

She gathered up the handkerchief, tucked it under her arm, and set forth.

CHAPTER 15

A Moonlit Performance

THE DOOR ESMERALDA HAD chosen opened into a kitchen. She was about to turn back when she spotted another door, also ajar, just past the cooking stove.

It was beyond this door that she found Irina. The girl lay fast asleep in bed, one hand dangling out from under the covers. Up close, the child's hand was enormous, and Esmeralda shuddered. How awful if Irina were to reach out and grab her, the way people grabbed pet dogs and cats. Esmeralda's impulse was to flee. She might have done so if she hadn't caught sight of Lyudmila.

The doll was sitting on a shelf near the bed. She was leaning against a stuffed toy bear whose gruff presence Esmeralda ignored. It was the doll's pink gown that she cared about. And the box next to the doll. "A box full of dresses," Esmeralda murmured.

She climbed up to the shelf and into the box. She fell onto a pile of soft fabric. Dresses and ribbons! Esmeralda lifted up a lavender silk gown with silver trim that gleamed in the moonlight from Irina's window. She clutched the dress to her and picked up another, this one pale blue with embroidered yellow flowers. And here was another — a white lace dress that made Esmeralda think of a snowflake.

"A box full of costumes!" she said.

She tossed the dresses and ribbons out of the box. When it was empty, she climbed out and unfolded the handkerchief. She piled the costumes on top of it, then tied the corners of the handkerchief together to form a bundle. She was about to push the bundle off the shelf when she remembered that Lyudmila was still wearing the pink dress.

The doll's gaze was uncomfortably lifelike. "I'm sorry," Esmeralda said as she untied Lyudmila's ribbon sash, "but we need all the costumes we can get."

Esmeralda slipped the dress over Lyudmila's head. The crystal beads dotting the skirt twinkled in the moonlight, and Esmeralda could not resist the impulse to try the dress on. It fit perfectly, as if it had been made for her.

"It will be the perfect costume for Clara," she said as she tied the sash. She twirled one . . . two . . . three times before she remembered that Fleur would be dancing the lead role in *Clara and the Mouse King*. Fleur would be the one to wear this beautiful dress.

Esmeralda slowed and let out a sigh.

She turned her head — and her blood went cold.

Irina was awake.

. . .

It occurred to Esmeralda that looking into the eyes of a human was not unlike looking into the eyes of another mouse. She found herself wondering what Irina was thinking. What *would* a little girl think if she woke up to find a mouse stealing her doll's clothes?

What would she think of a mouse *wearing* her doll's clothes?

Irina yawned. Her eyes started to close, then opened again.

She was half asleep, Esmeralda realized. Irina probably thought she was dreaming.

How should a mouse in a little girl's dream behave? Surely not like the mice in *The Nutcracker*, running about and frightening poor Clara.

Esmeralda didn't want to frighten Irina. If she was going to be in Irina's dream, it had better be a quiet dream. She needed Irina to go back to sleep.

In Esmeralda's mind, an imaginary celesta

played the delicate notes that began the "Dance of the Sugar Plum Fairy."

In their new scenario, it would be Clara Silvermouse who danced to this lovely music. Fleur would dance the role of Clara on the Mariinsky stage. But now, here in Irina's room, Esmeralda pretended that *she* was Clara Silvermouse. She let the music play in her mind and danced, taking tiny, mincing steps. She looked up and saw Irina's mouth twitch in a sleepy smile. The imaginary celesta played on, and Esmeralda danced on tiptoe, aware of her costume floating around her as she pirouetted, aware that the crystal beads were shooting out sparkles of reflected moonlight. She danced as she had at the café, letting her arms and her legs *and* her tail move to the music. Gradually, she forgot about Irina. The music cast its spell and Esmeralda felt as if she really were Clara Silvermouse, dancing by moonlight because she was in love with the mouse king.

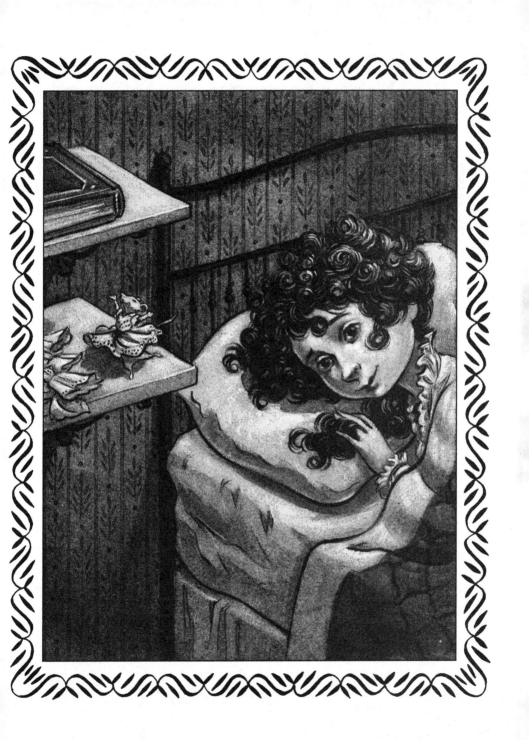

Only when the imaginary celesta had spun out its tune did Esmeralda remember who and where she was.

Only then did she remember that she had an audience.

Only then did she see that Irina was asleep.

CHAPTER 16

Sasha and a Sword Fight

THE BUNDLE OF COSTUMES was heavier than Esmeralda had expected it would be. She pushed it off the shelf, then pulled it along the floor. She had to push and pull and lift the bundle when she reached the door to the kitchen just to get it over the doorjamb. How would she ever manage to hoist the costumes into the coat hem?

She had just reached the cast-iron stove when Irina woke up.

"Papa?" Then louder: "Papa!"

Esmeralda darted under the stove. There wasn't time to grab the bundle. She watched as a pair of slippered feet shuffled across the kitchen floor. "What is it, Irina?"

"There was a mouse in my room, Papa! She was dancing! She was wearing a dress!"

"Silly girl! Mice don't wear clothes."

"This one did!"

"You had a dream, Irinushka. You know we don't have mice in our house. Sasha would never allow it."

Sasha again, thought Esmeralda. Who was Sasha?

"I saw the mouse, Papa! It was a ballerina mouse!"

"It's time to go back to sleep!"

"You don't believe me!"

"You're tired! Tell you what: I'll go and see if Sasha's outside. She's probably tired of hunting—good and ready to come in. Would you like it if she climbed into bed with you?"

"Yes, but—!"

Mikhail Danilovich shuffled back through the kitchen and into the sitting room.

Esmeralda heard a door open. She felt a rush of cold air.

"Ah! There you are!" said Mikhail Danilovich.

Esmeralda heard the door close again. A moment later, Irina's father crossed the kitchen and reentered the bedroom.

"Sasha!" said Irina.

Esmeralda frowned. Surely Mikhail Danilovich had been alone!

He was definitely alone when, after saying a final good night to Irina, he passed again through the kitchen.

She heard a door close. She waited for the house to grow quiet again, then resumed her struggles with the handkerchief bundle. It caught on something as she dragged it along. She had to work to unhitch it from a nail in a floorboard, and the effort chased the mystery of Sasha from her mind.

And then a chill came over her—a feeling of danger so extreme it temporarily paralyzed her. She struggled to remember how to turn her head. When she did, she saw two golden eyes in the darkness, and in that moment, she knew exactly who—or *what*—Sasha was.

Golden eyes, black fur, and white teeth! The cat sprang at her, and Esmeralda ran. Through the door to the living room. Across the floor toward Mikhail Danilovich's coat. At the last minute, she changed her mind and made a dash for the sewing basket. She reached for the tulle skirt. If she could climb into the basket . . .

Something clapped down on her back. Something sharp dug into her flesh, pushing her to the floor, dragging her backward.

The cat let go. Esmeralda ran forward again. This time the cat's paw swiped at her from the side, sending her tumbling. She righted herself, determined to run back to the basket. The paw came down like a wall in front of her. As Esmeralda tried to scramble over it, she felt herself lifted up in the air. A hot, dreadful smell of fish engulfed her, even as Sasha's sharp teeth pressed into her fur.

"Let me go!" Esmeralda screamed.

She fell, her feet moving even before she hit the floor. This time the cat's paw came down on Esmeralda's tail, and she looked up to find Sasha leering at her. She tried to pull her tail free, and Sasha's eyes flickered with interest. The cat lifted her paw, letting Esmeralda run a few steps before she trapped her again.

Esmeralda thought of Conrad's older brother, who had been caught and killed by a cat only last year. Nobody talked about it much, but Esmeralda thought now of things she had heard:

The cat must have played with him . . . they always play with you . . .

They never found his body . . .

Probably eaten alive . . .

151

The cat's jaws closed around Esmeralda again. She tried to scream, but all that came out was a whimper.

"*Please,* let me go."

Sasha loosed her jaws, but she pressed her paw against Esmeralda's tail, still trapping her. The cat bared her teeth in a cruel smile. "What will you give me if I let you go?"

Esmeralda drew in her breath. What *could* she give to a cat?

From the corner of her eye, she could see the sewing needle tucked into the tulle of the ballet costume. She said, "There's something in the basket! I'll get it for you."

The cat sneered. "There's nothing in the basket. I had fish for supper. I'll have mouse for dessert."

Esmeralda grabbed her tail with both hands and yanked it free. She ran for the basket. She grabbed the sewing needle. She pulled it out and whirled around.

Sasha gave a derisive laugh. "Look at you! Just like one of the tsar's soldiers. Too bad he doesn't need a mouse in his army."

Esmeralda waved her sword. "Get back!"

And before Sasha could get closer, Esmeralda darted forward and jabbed the cat in the nose.

Sasha gave a yowl.

Esmeralda jabbed again, stabbing Sasha in the jaw.

Another yowl.

Now Sasha was hissing and arching her back. She batted the needle with her paw, but Esmeralda jabbed again and the cat gave another wail.

A door flew open. Taking advantage of the distraction, Esmeralda dropped the needle and ran. She scrambled up the tulle skirt and under the basket lid just as Sasha threw herself against it. The cat's paws pushed their way under the lid, clawing at the tulle.

Mikhail Danilovich said, "No! Bad cat! Stop it, Sasha!"

The clawing stopped.

"Ow! Ouch! What is wrong with you?" exclaimed Mikhail Danilovich.

Esmeralda heard footsteps. She heard a door open and felt a blast of cold air.

"Get out, you beast!" said Mikhail Danilovich, and the door slammed shut.

"What is going on?" It was Irina's mother.

"The cat went crazy! I had to put her outside. She was trying to get into your sewing basket—"

"My sewing basket!"

The basket shook and the lid was thrown open. Esmeralda scrambled to hide.

"Light the lamp, Misha, so I can see. I'll strangle that cat if she's wrecked this costume!"

The room filled with light. Irina's mother lifted the dress out of the basket and turned it this way and that, running her hands over the fabric. Esmeralda, caught inside a fold, gripped the tulle and prayed she wouldn't be seen.

Irina's mother said, "It looks all right. What a mercy! It was foolish of me to leave the basket open."

She began folding the costume, gathering up the tulle—and Esmeralda. She laid the costume back inside the sewing basket, and Esmeralda felt the weight of the fabric pushing down on her. She heard a sharp *click*.

"What a night! First a mouse, and now our own cat," said Irina's father.

"A mouse!"

"A dancing ballerina mouse in a dress . . . something from Irina's dream."

"Goodness! The dreams that girl has!"

Both parents were laughing. Esmeralda heard their door close, the murmur of their voices, and then silence.

She pushed at the tulle. Sasha was outside. If she

could get out of the sewing basket, she might be able to get the costumes into the coat after all. This was her last chance.

The fabric blocked her on all sides. Esmeralda clawed at it, trying to pull herself forward, not at all sure that she was heading anywhere useful. At one point, the ribbon of Lyudmila's dress came undone. Esmeralda pulled off the doll's dress and left it behind.

At last she broke free of the fabric. Her nose bumped into the side of the basket. Esmeralda climbed up to the top and pushed on the lid.

It didn't move.

She circled the rim of the basket, pushing on the lid at every point. It would not budge, and Esmeralda remembered the *click* she had heard.

The basket had a latch.

She was a prisoner!

CHAPTER 17

A Terror of Mice

HOW COULD A dancing mouse wearing a dress be anything but a dream? That was Papa's opinion, and at the time, Irina had almost agreed with him.

But the morning brought a discovery. "Lyudmila's dresses are missing!" Irina told her mother.

Mama said, "I'm sure they're somewhere." She was rushing about, getting ready for work. Irina was to go with her parents today. Mama added, "Madame Federova says that the director is coming to look at the costumes this morning. You must sit quietly and not bother anyone."

"I'll be quiet." Irina slipped a bit of her bread into her pocket for the mouse that lived under the cupboard in the costume department. Could it be the same mouse as the one in her room last night? Could there be two dancing mice?

Mama said, "Be a good girl. Sweep the kitchen while I put together some food for our lunch."

That was how Irina found Lyudmila's dresses. The broom swept a small white bundle out from under the kitchen table. Puzzled, Irina untied the bundle. "Mama, look!"

Her mother barely glanced at the dresses. "I knew you would find them!"

"But how did they get here? Whose handkerchief is this?"

"Hurry up! It's time to go!" said Papa.

Irina left the handkerchief and the dresses on the kitchen table. Papa helped her into her coat. He put on his own coat, pulling off a string that had caught on a button.

He opened the front door, and Sasha pushed her way into the apartment. She made a beeline for the sewing basket, but Mama snatched it up. She scolded the cat, "You be good while we're away, Sasha! No more mischief!"

The rush to get ready at home was nothing compared to the bustle Irina and her mother found in the costume department. Even before they entered the large room where the seamstresses did their work, they could hear Madame Federova scolding people.

"You there! Look lively and sew on that last bit of trim!"

"You're still working on those trousers? It's been three days!"

"No, no, no! The skirt is much too short! You'll have to do it over!"

Madame Federova was a short, fat woman whose shiny black braid was pinned in a tight coil on the top of her head. She wore a striped apron with pockets that held a measuring tape, scissors, and other tools. She liked to be organized, even when surrounded by chaos.

She saw Irina's mother and hurried over. "Ah! There you are, Sonya Borisovna! Please tell me that you've finished the Sugar Plum Fairy costume!"

"Very nearly, Madame!"

"Well, get it up on the form — quickly! I want to have *something* decent to show the director."

There were at least a dozen dressmaker's dummies of various sizes in the costume department. This morning, all but two were already dressed and ready for Monsieur Vsevolozhsky's visit. Mama unlatched her basket and lifted out the Sugar Plum Fairy costume. She draped it over the larger of the undressed forms. She smoothed the bodice with her hand and tugged gently at the tulle skirt.

"The dress is too big," said Irina. "Look! It's sagging!"

Mama said, "This form is smaller than Mademoiselle dell'Era. I'll have to—"

"*Bonjour*, Madame Federova!" The voice of the theater director boomed from the door.

Irina did what she was supposed to do. She found a chair and sat down.

"I've brought a surprise guest," said Monsieur Vsevolozhsky. "Monsieur Tchaikovsky was asking me how the costumes were coming along, so I invited him to come see."

The great composer himself! The seamstresses smoothed their aprons and stood at attention next to the costumed forms. Madame Federova curtsied. She said, "We are honored, Monsieur Tchaikovsky. It is our greatest pleasure to make the costumes for *The Nutcracker*. Such a charming story."

"Yes, well. It certainly is a strange story," said Monsieur Tchaikovsky. "I wasn't especially fond of it at first, but I have come around."

"Everyone will love the music," said Monsieur Vsevolozhsky.

"And the costumes, I am sure," said Monsieur Tchaikovsky. "What have we here?"

"This costume is for the Arabian dance in the second act," said Madame Federova.

"Very nice!" said Monsieur Tchaikovsky.

"And this costume," said Madame Federova, with a proud flourish of her hand, "will be worn by the Sugar Plum Fairy."

Irina sat up straighter in her chair. Mama was by far the best seamstress at the Mariinsky, and Madame Federova was justifiably proud of the work she did.

Monsieur Tchaikovsky's eyes widened as he took in the beautiful costume. "Why, it's splendid!" he said. Then he tilted his head. "Except . . . does it seem as if it's a bit crooked?"

The dress wasn't crooked. It was only that it

was too big for the form. Irina hoped Mama would explain.

Instead, Madame Federova said, "You are absolutely right, Monsieur. The costume needs an adjustment." She gave Irina's mother a meaningful look. "Sonya Borisovna, if you would fetch some pins . . . ?"

Mama hurried over to her sewing basket. She pulled out her pincushion—

And screamed!

Heads turned. Everyone saw the mouse leap out of the basket.

The mouse ran to the left.

"Look out!" someone shouted.

"Catch it! Catch it!" shouted someone else.

The mouse ran to the right. Another seamstress shrieked and shoved her chair in its path.

The mouse ran around in a circle, then turned and raced up onto Monsieur Tchaikovsky's polished black shoe. The composer screamed and kicked his

foot, sending the mouse flying through the air. It hit the front of a cupboard and slid to the floor.

Irina ran over. She was just about to pick up the stunned mouse when someone shoved her out of the way.

"Let me get it!"

Konstantin Grigorovich Gurkin wielded his broom. He raised it high, ready to strike.

"Run!" Irina shouted.

The mouse lifted its head. . . .

"Run!"

Whack! The broom came down, but the mouse was gone — safe under the cupboard.

Gurkin glared at Irina.

She looked away and saw Monsieur Tchaikovsky crouched atop a chair.

"Oh! Oh! Oh!" he gasped.

Monsieur Vsevolozhsky took his arm. "Please, Pyotr Ilich! Sit down!"

"Is it—is it gone?" said the composer. His face was completely white.

"Yes! Yes, the mouse is gone!"

Monsieur Vsevolozhsky helped the trembling composer down from his perch. Monsieur Tchaikovsky collapsed into the chair.

"Clear away, everyone! Give him some air!" said the director.

The composer buried his face in his hands. "Please forgive me. I—I'm afraid I have a terror of mice. When I was a child, I used to have nightmares."

"My dear friend, what can I get you? Some water? Perhaps some brandy . . . ?" Monsieur Vsevolozhsky's voice was soothing as he spoke to Monsieur Tchaikovsky.

But a moment later, the director beckoned to Madame Federova. He spoke to her in a sharp undertone. "Send someone to find the chief custodian. Tell him that I want to speak to him in my office!"

Madame Federova nodded and beckoned to one of the seamstresses. The young woman listened to Madame Federova's whispered instructions and hurried out of the room.

Meanwhile, the director had returned his attention to Monsieur Tchaikovsky. He patted him on the shoulder. "I don't know how I can apologize enough! I cannot think how such a thing could have happened, and I assure you that measures will be taken so that nothing like this will ever happen again. Come with me now. . . ." Monsieur Vsevolozhsky took the composer by the arm, helping him rise. He steered him out of the room.

When they were gone, Madame Federova threw up her arms. "Of all things to have in your sewing basket, Sonya Borisovna! Whatever possessed you to bring *mice* to the theater?"

Mama looked almost as white as Monsieur Tchaikovsky. "I didn't! We don't have mice at home!"

"Let me see that basket!" said Gurkin. He rummaged through Mama's sewing supplies, pulling out scissors and spools of thread and packets of needles and bits of fabric, tossing everything aside. "It's time to get rid of these vermin, once and for all!" he growled.

When the basket was empty, he glowered at Mama and said, "It appears that all the mice have escaped from the nest."

At this, Mama burst into tears.

Madame Federova gave Gurkin a fierce look. She said, "I am quite sure that Sonya Borisovna did not mean to have a nest of mice in her sewing basket."

Irina said, "There wasn't a nest! And it was only one mouse!"

But nobody paid any attention to her. Gurkin stalked out of the room. Madame Federova comforted Mama, helping her into a chair. The other seamstresses returned to their work.

Irina began picking up Mama's sewing supplies, putting them back into the basket. Suddenly, she gave a start. There, among the scraps of fabric Gurkin had tossed onto the table, was Lyudmila's pink dress — the same dress that had been worn by the mouse in her dream!

She turned to show Mama, but stopped, surprised to see Papa enter the room. His expression was grim.

Mama looked at him with red-rimmed eyes. "Misha, what is it?"

Papa said, "I've been let go."

Mama gasped. "You've lost your job?"

Papa continued. "The director is holding me responsible for what happened. Everyone knows the theater has a mouse problem. I've been trying to solve it for years without success. Monsieur Vsevolozhsky is being kind enough to give me two weeks' pay, but I'm to leave immediately."

"He should fire me! The mouse was in my sewing basket!" said Mama.

Madame Federova protested. "I wouldn't allow it if he did fire you, Sonya Borisovna. You're the best seamstress here. Listen, go home with your husband now. But come back tomorrow."

Mama was crying again, and Madame Federova, normally a rather cold person, looked as if she might cry, too. "Everything will be fine," she said. "You'll see."

Irina couldn't see how anything could be fine. She had never seen Mama cry in front of other people. And she wasn't sure she had ever seen her father look so unhappy.

Papa said, "Come, Irina. We'll go home now."

She could almost hear his next thought—that he would go home, and not come back.

Poor Papa!

She looked down at Lyudmila's pink dress, now crumpled in her hand. She thought of the mouse, remembering the angry *whack* of Gurkin's broom and the custodian's angry vow to get rid of the theater's mice *once and for all.*

Poor mouse!

CHAPTER 18

The New Mousetrap

"AT LEAST WE HAVE the new scenario," Conrad said to Esmeralda and Gringoire one morning in the attic some days later. "We have to be happy about that, even if our plans for sets and costumes haven't worked out quite as we hoped."

While Esmeralda had been battling Sasha at the Chernovs' home, Gringoire and Conrad and a small contingent of mice had carried out their own expedition, transporting the set-design illustrations from the director's office to the mouse stage.

Unfortunately, Madame Giselle had said *no* to the mouse-size sets when she saw them the next morning. The paintings were too distracting, she said. And so the beautiful set designs were now propped up backward against the wall behind the stage.

As for the costumes, not only had Esmeralda failed to retrieve them, but her actions had caused Irina's father to lose his job. It was her fault that the Mariinsky Theater now had a new chief custodian.

Within hours of Mikhail Danilovich Chernov's departure from the theater, his successor, Konstantin Grigorovich Gurkin, had begun outlining proposals for treating what he called the theater's *rodent infestation*. So far, these proposals had included cats (rejected because they made people sneeze), poison (rejected because the mice would die inside the walls, causing a terrible smell), and dogs (rejected because these animals were expert rat-catchers, not mouse-catchers).

"I *am* glad about the scenario," said Esmeralda. "But I'm worried about Gurkin."

"Don't you worry. The man's got lots to say, but so far it's all just words."

It was strange that Conrad should say that. For just then, they heard Gurkin's gravelly voice. "We'll start up here!"

The attic stairs creaked. The mice quickly withdrew behind Gringoire's stacks of books. They couldn't see, but from the sound of things, there were several people with Gurkin. The mice heard a clatter as something was set on the floor.

"So, here's how the new mousetrap works," said Gurkin.

The mice exchanged looks.

"You simply drop in the bait like so," Gurkin continued. "Notice that I've chosen an especially fragrant cheese, so that the unsuspecting rodent cannot help but be attracted by the smell. The mouse climbs into this hole at the top, falls in, and there you have it!"

"You mean, we put poison in the cheese?" said another man.

Gurkin chuckled. "No need for that. As you can see, these sharp spikes prevent the rodent from getting out the way it came in."

"What about that hole at the bottom?" asked a third man.

"Ha! That just happens to be the most ingenious part of this mousetrap. It's what makes our job easy. You simply slide a thin board underneath like so, pick up the entire mousetrap, slide the board out, and shake the rodent into this pail. Slam the lid down on the pail and you're done! Rebait this trap and move on to the next one. Simple, fast, and effective!"

"What do we do with the mouse in the pail?"

"Mice, my good man. You can fit quite a few in there before you dispose of them."

"Dispose of them how?"

"However you like. Drown them . . . chloroform them . . . crush them with a rock . . ."

"Can we throw them in the furnace?"

"Well, there could be a smell. Still, it might be worth a try. I guess we'll know when they catch fire, eh?" Gurkin laughed again. Then he and the other custodians tromped back down the stairs.

A sound halfway between a gasp and a sob escaped Esmeralda. "What a horrible man!"

But Gringoire was pragmatic. "Let's go have a look."

The new mousetrap was a domed metal cage with narrowly spaced bars. It was about five times as tall as a mouse and had a round, funnel-shaped hole at the top. The hole ended in a circle of spikes that pointed down toward another hole in the metal plate that formed the bottom of the mousetrap.

Gringoire said, "As traps go, it *is* rather clever.

You can slide in easily enough, but you'll be impaled if you try to climb back out."

"How about the hole at the bottom?" asked Conrad.

Gringoire shook his head. "No good escaping that way unless you can get through the attic floor. Maybe we can lift the trap."

Together they tried, but the three of them couldn't even push it sideways.

Esmeralda said, "This is awful! If they're all baited with that smelly cheese, we'll have a terrible time keeping the children away!"

Gringoire said, "Not only that, but the bars are too close together for us to get at the bait. We're not going to get any food from these traps."

"We'll have to increase the number of scrounge patrols," said Conrad.

"Or hope that *Clara and the Mouse King* will be a success," said Gringoire. "If the ballet company can start collecting food for admission again, we'll be all right. In the meantime, I think we'll have to propose food rationing."

"That's not going to make anybody very happy," said Conrad.

Esmeralda thought of Fleur, who never went on scrounge patrol but always felt she ought to have more than everyone else. The *prima ballerina* wasn't the only member of the Russian Mouse Ballet Company who felt so entitled. It was going to take quite a few extra scrounge patrols to keep the dancers from complaining.

"I can hunt for food more often," she said. "Now that I'm not playing Clara, I'm not rehearsing as much. I'll have more time."

"Listen to you," said Conrad. "You're nearly killed by a cat, Russia's greatest composer kicks you across a room, and you're already planning to head out for more danger."

"When you put it like that . . ." Esmeralda said, laughing.

Perhaps she was being a bit foolhardy. But she was partly—if not mostly—to blame for the current situation. She wouldn't feel right if she didn't do everything she could to help.

Besides, there was a note of admiration in Conrad's voice that she found enormously cheering.

CHAPTER 19

A Surprise Gift

WITHIN DAYS, EVERYONE had been warned about the new mousetraps. The Mariinsky mice understood that for the time being, the food brought in by the scrounge patrols would have to suffice, and that they must subsist on a small daily food ration from the community stockpiles.

Scrounge patrols were sent out every night, and Esmeralda's brother volunteered to collect and guard the food they brought back. Gringoire was on duty one evening when Esmeralda and Maksim returned from a food-hunting expedition. Esmeralda had found a small radish, and Maksim half a rubbery carrot.

"There just wasn't much to find tonight," Maksim explained.

"Go ahead and add the food to the pile," said Gringoire in a dull voice.

"What's wrong?" Esmeralda asked.

Her brother sighed. "I'm tired of complaints about the short rations. You'd think the mice would be grateful to have food to eat—that they wouldn't be picky. But no, we'll hand out food in the morning, and the mice will be sure to complain that they don't like what they're getting."

"It's hard to blame them!" Esmeralda had taken a test nibble of her radish. Her tongue still burned from the taste of it.

Gringoire said, "To make matters worse, Franz has been stirring up all kinds of fears and bad feelings. I can't tell you how many mice have asked me if it's true that the rations are going to run out in a few days. I've had mothers and fathers come to me in tears, begging me to figure out how to outwit the new traps. Nobody can blame them for worrying about their children getting caught, but Franz has convinced them that their children are going to starve to death!"

Esmeralda said, "I think Fleur is almost as bad. I heard her talking with Franz the other day. *She* was saying how it wasn't fair that the dancers have to work in such conditions, and *he* was saying how they really needed to do something about the situation."

Gringoire frowned. "I'm afraid Franz will do something rash! He said to me today, 'Gurkin wants to exterminate us! We mice got rid of the last custodian! Now let's get rid of Gurkin!'"

"How would he do that?" Esmeralda wondered aloud.

"I have no idea. But I wish Franz could understand that there are worse things than what we've got now.

People are always thinking of new ways to torture mice. Before you know it, someone's going to invent an electrocuting mousetrap."

"What's that?" asked Maksim.

"Trust me. We don't want to find out!" said Gringoire.

The food shortage could not be allowed to affect rehearsals, especially because the late change in the scenario meant extra work for many of the dancers—particularly Fleur and Conrad, who needed to learn completely new choreography.

As for Esmeralda, Madame Giselle asked if she would be willing to supervise the children at rehearsals. Esmeralda was happy to be useful, and she found out that helping the children gave her insight into her struggles with her tail.

"You must pretend that the training ribbon isn't there," she told the children. "Wrap your tail around tight and concentrate on not letting it move."

"But my tail wants to dance to the music!" said one of the young dancers.

Esmeralda hid a smile. "I know that's how it feels! But this is ballet. Just as you've worked to perfect your *port de bras*, and just as you've taught your feet all of the basic positions, you must learn to control your tail. This time, as you perform those steps, concentrate on not letting your tail twitch. Success will come to you if you practice."

Esmeralda could give this advice with some confidence. Though she still practiced with the training ribbon during morning class and at afternoon rehearsals, she also practiced in secret *without* the training ribbon. At first, she worked on the relatively simple children's dances she would perform in *Clara and the Mouse King*. When she had mastered these, she began practicing more difficult dances, including those that Fleur would be performing in the role of Clara. It wasn't easy: concentrating so hard on her tail tended to interfere with what Madame Giselle called *musicality*. This awareness of rhythm and melody came easily to Esmeralda when she danced at the Balalaika Café; if only she could feel that same awareness when she danced ballet!

One afternoon, she did feel it. She and the children were at rehearsal. Madame Giselle stood in front of the stage, watching them dance. Esmeralda was wearing her training ribbon, but she was following her own advice and pretending that she wasn't. She was concentrating on not letting her tail move even as she listened to the music. The orchestra was playing; it was thrilling to dance to the actual score, not the piano version they had been hearing for weeks. Esmeralda crossed the stage, performing a series of *chaîné* turns. Perhaps it was only because the choreography was simple, but suddenly she felt something close to what she always felt at the Balalaika Café. She could feel the music flowing through her body.

"Très bien!" Madame Giselle called out.

That Esmeralda's tail popped out of the ribbon a moment later had less to do with the ballet mistress's words of praise than it had to do with a distraction in front of the stage. The girl mouse to Esmeralda's right stopped in the middle of a turn. "Look!" cried the girl mouse, and Esmeralda bumped into her. The boy mouse to Esmeralda's left bumped into Esmeralda. The music went on, but the dancing came to a halt.

The arrival of Fleur and Conrad at rehearsal did not usually cause a commotion. But today, there were gasps from all around.

Esmeralda was astonished to see Fleur wearing a dress—a pale pink dress with crystal beads that sparkled in the light from the candles in front of the stage.

No doubt reveling in the attention, Fleur performed several *piqué* turns. She came to a stop in

front of Madame Giselle and dipped herself in an elegant stage curtsy.

"What is the meaning of this?" Madame Giselle's voice was sharp.

"It's a costume!" Fleur pirouetted. The beads on the dress twinkled, inspiring *ooh*s and *aah*s from the mice on stage.

Madame Giselle said coldly, "I suppose this so-called *costume* is the reason why you are late for rehearsal?"

Conrad said, "Not *costume* — *costumes*!"

Esmeralda saw that her cousin had been dragging a familiar white cloth bundle across the floor.

Conrad now began untying the bundle. He said, "Our apologies, Madame. We couldn't help being late. When we found these costumes upstairs, we felt we must bring them to show you." He lifted the corners of the handkerchief, revealing a rainbow of colors.

There were squeals of excitement from those on

stage. Esmeralda's fellow dancers jumped down and crowded around the pile of costumes.

"Let me see! Let me see!" they cried as they snatched up the dresses and ribbons.

"Oh, look at this! Just right for the party scene!"

"These white dresses will be perfect for the 'Waltz of the Snowflakes'!"

"Say, we soldiers can wear these ribbons, can't we? Like military sashes."

Now the mice were trying on the costumes. Madame Giselle had to shout three times for attention.

The mice, in varying states of dress, fell silent.

"We do not need costumes in our ballet!" said Madame Giselle.

Her stern declaration was met with a chorus of protests. Fleur pushed her way forward. "We may not need them, but we want them. *I* want them," she said. "And I am going to wear this dress when I dance the role of Clara!"

Madame Giselle looked taken aback, but she adopted a softer tone. "Now then, my dear, the costumes will be a distraction for the audience. Furthermore, it will interfere with your ability to express yourself artistically—"

"I disagree! I look beautiful in this costume—I *feel* beautiful. That's sure to improve my performance." Fleur tossed her head. "If you won't let me wear this costume, Madame, I won't dance!"

Conrad cleared his throat. He said, "I won't dance either, Madame. And I'll wager a guess that everyone here feels the same way."

"Oh, yes! Yes!" cried the other mice. "We must wear the costumes!"

"But—but—!" spluttered the ballet mistress.

Fleur folded her arms. "Furthermore, I insist that we use the sets that Conrad and Gringoire obtained for us! It will be easier to dance with costumes *and* sets."

"They'll make the story feel more real to the audience *and* to us dancers. We'll dance with much more emotion!" Conrad added, throwing a look in Esmeralda's direction.

The other dancers agreed. "Yes! *Please*, Madame Giselle!"

Esmeralda held her breath, sure that the ballet mistress would not give in.

But Madame Giselle threw up her hands. "Very well," she conceded.

Rehearsal could not continue, not until every dancer had found a costume.

The dresses were too big for the little girl mice. "Never mind," Esmeralda told them. "I won't wear a dress either, but we can wear different colored ribbons. And just think! By the time we put on our next ballet, you'll have grown. You'll be able to wear these beautiful costumes!"

Conrad walked up to her, looking resplendent in a red military sash. He said, "I think I've tied it too tight."

Esmeralda adjusted the ribbon and regarded him with pleasure. "You look just like a mouse king! Except I think you need a crown; we'll have to make one. Oh, Conrad! Wherever did you find the costumes?"

He said, "They were under a cupboard in the costume department. They were wrapped up in your handkerchief. You're sure you didn't leave them there?"

She shook her head. "I told you! I left them at Irina's home. I wonder . . ." Esmeralda thought of the food Irina had left in the costume department. Was it possible that Irina had also left the costumes as a gift for the mice?

When she suggested this to Conrad, he shrugged. "That's a little hard to believe. But there they were, nonetheless. I was gathering everything up so I could bring the costumes to rehearsal when Fleur showed up. She took one look at that pink dress and put it on. She insisted on coming with me to confront Madame Giselle." Conrad grinned. "I suppose it's lucky she came by just then. When our *prima ballerina* wants something, she makes sure to get it! Can you believe it, Esmeralda? We're going to have sets and costumes, after all!"

CHAPTER 20

Kind to Mice

WHEN IRINA FIRST SAW the trap on the floor of the costume department, she thought it was a cage. "It's for catching mice," Mama told her.

When she and Mama got home, Irina drew a picture of the mousetrap for Papa.

He said, "See this hole? The mouse climbs in and can't escape. The custodians have to get the mouse out through this other hole in the bottom."

"Then what?" Irina asked.

"Then they'll kill it."

"That's mean, Papa! How could anybody kill a mouse?"

"That's what mousetraps are for, Irina," said Papa. Perhaps he sensed her horror, for he added gently, "I suppose you'd like something a bit more . . . humane?"

"What does *humane* mean?"

"It means being kind to the mice." Papa looked at the drawing again. "Has Gurkin caught very many mice in his new traps?" he wondered aloud.

Irina shook her head. "I don't think so. Gurkin says his traps have chased the mice out of the theater. He says they've moved out because they can't get free food anymore."

Papa looked dubious. "No more mice! What do you think?"

Irina wasn't sure. Today was the first day since Papa had lost his job that she had been able to go to the theater with Mama. She had left the bundle of

Lyudmila's doll clothes under the mouse cupboard. She said, "I hope the mice are still there."

Papa laughed. "I suppose it makes me a pretty bad custodian, but I hope the same thing. I confess, I always enjoyed seeing how those clever mice outwitted my traps."

"You're *not* a bad custodian, Papa!"

Her father didn't answer, and Irina knew he was thinking about losing his job. She had overheard Mama and Papa talking about how hard things were going to be this winter. There would be less coal for the fire. Even now, the sitting room was chilly; Irina was wearing two sweaters! Mama had started making stew without meat because she couldn't afford to shop at the butcher's. And Irina couldn't go to her school anymore. "We'll find you a new school after Christmas," Mama had told her. "One that doesn't cost as much." Irina hadn't cried when Mama told her about school. Nor had she cried when Mama said they couldn't have a Christmas tree this year and that she shouldn't expect many presents. But she had wanted to cry.

Irina knew it was much worse for Papa. He felt responsible for everything that had happened to them. She said, "You're the best custodian in the world. What's more, you're kind! You're kind to everyone!"

His smile was wry. He said, "Even to mice?"

She hugged him. "Especially to mice!"

CHAPTER 21

Fulcrum and Lever

PLEASE, FLEUR! PLEASE be quiet!" begged Esmeralda.

The Russian Mouse Ballet Company's *prima ballerina* lay on her stomach inside the mousetrap in the costume department, her face buried in her arms. She was sobbing uncontrollably. Which was marginally better than shouting. Which was what Fleur *had* been doing in the dark early hours of the morning—when Esmeralda, Conrad, and Maksim, returning from scrounge patrol, had heard her cries: *Help! Help! Somebody, help!*

They had tried to get her out of the trap by forming a chain of mice—Maksim holding on to Conrad's feet, Conrad holding on to Esmeralda's, and Esmeralda reaching down into the trap. "Grab hold of my hands!" Esmeralda had told Fleur.

Maksim had pulled on Conrad's feet, and Conrad had pulled on Esmeralda's, and Esmeralda had lifted Fleur up from the bottom of the trap. Things had looked promising until Fleur had scraped her arm on a sharp spike. She had shrieked and kicked, and Conrad had lost hold of Esmeralda, and now Esmeralda was inside the trap as well.

"Hush, Fleur! Somebody might hear you!" said Esmeralda. At this hour, the Mariinsky was more or less empty, but there would be a custodian on duty. "Conrad and Maksim have gone to get help," she added, trying to sound more hopeful than she felt.

Fleur rolled over onto her back. "I was hungry. I just wanted something to eat!"

All the Mariinsky mice were hungry, but nobody

else had ignored the warnings about the mousetraps. How could Fleur have been so foolish?

Esmeralda kept these thoughts to herself. She said, "Look! Here they are now!"

Maksim and Conrad had brought Gringoire with them. Maksim reached through the bars of the mousetrap to grasp Esmeralda's hands. "Conrad says your brother will come up with a way to get you out," he told her.

Indeed, Gringoire was already circling the mousetrap, studying the bottom edge. He stopped suddenly and said, "Do you see this here?"

Everyone came to look.

Gringoire said, "There's a crack in the floor-boards. It goes under the mousetrap. If we could find something long and narrow, we could wedge it into the crack."

"What good is that?"

Gringoire ignored Maksim's question. His eyes narrowed, as they always did when he was thinking hard. "We need something long and rigid. We'll also need something to use as a fulcrum."

Conrad said, "What's a *full of crumb*—or whatever you said?"

"A *fulcrum* is the point on which a lever rests."

"What's a *lever*?" asked Maksim.

Gringoire explained. "It's a simple machine used for lifting. 'Give me a lever long enough and a place to stand, and I will move the Earth,' said Archimedes. Only we mice are not going to move the Earth. We are going to use a lever to move this mousetrap."

Esmeralda had never heard of Archimedes, but she guessed that he or she must have written one of the books in the attic. She said, "Long and rigid . . . like a broomstick?"

"Too heavy. We must be able to carry our lever here, and we have to be able to wedge the end of it under the mousetrap."

"A butter knife!" said Conrad. "There's one that fell behind a chair in the tsar's salon."

Gringoire shook his head. "Too short."

Esmeralda closed her eyes, trying to think of something long and rigid—something light that mice could carry. "What about Monsieur Drigo's conducting baton?"

"Perfect! And I think we can use a thread spool for the fulcrum."

"There's a whole pile of them over there," said Conrad, gesturing to a table on the other side of the costume department.

"We also need more mice," said Gringoire. "As many as we can find."

"We'll have to wake them up," said Conrad.

"Watch out for the custodian!" said Esmeralda.

"Right!" said her brother. "Gurkin's on duty tonight. But don't you worry. I think he's given up checking the mousetraps. I've heard him bragging about how they're always empty. He seems to be under the mistaken impression that we mice have moved out of the theater."

• • •

Not nearly soon enough for comfort, Gringoire and the others returned with the necessary supplies. They had also roused a team of rescuers, among them Madame Giselle.

The mice gathered around as Esmeralda's brother gave directions. He pointed to where he wanted them to place the thread spool. "We'll put the fulcrum here. I think we'd better turn it on its side. That way the lever will be less likely to slip off. Madame Giselle, you hold the spool in place."

Though wild-eyed with worry, the ballet mistress did as she was told.

Gringoire went on. "The rest of you need to place the lever on top of the fulcrum."

The mice set to work positioning the baton, following Gringoire's directions: "That's it! No, no! Move it a little more this way!"

Once the baton was in place, Gringoire and Maksim maneuvered its tip into the crack beneath the mousetrap. "Next we're going to apply a downward force on the high end of the lever," said Gringoire. "Climb up now, as many as can fit. I'll make sure this end stays wedged under the trap."

One by one, the mice climbed onto the baton. They crouched along its length, balancing like birds on a telegraph wire.

Nothing happened.

Gringoire said, "Try crowding all together, as close to the far end of the lever as possible."

"There isn't room!" Even as Conrad said this, he slipped. Just in time, he grabbed the baton. He hung there, dangling above the ground.

"That's the way! If more of you hang on like Conrad, you can shift your collective center of gravity away from the fulcrum."

Maksim and two other mice dropped down into a dangling position. Above them, the other mice pushed their way to the end of the baton.

"The mousetrap is moving!" shrieked Fleur.

Sure enough, as the mouse end of the lever descended, the mousetrap end moved up.

"Shift your weight just a bit more, and I think we'll have it," said Gringoire.

"Shh!"

Everyone froze, listening. Someone was whistling the "Dance of the Sugar Plum Fairy."

Gurkin, thought Esmeralda. And then . . .

Only one mouse let go of the baton—but that was enough. The mousetrap end of the lever bumped to the ground, jolting the mice at the other end into the air.

The whistling stopped abruptly. The door of the costume department creaked open.

The mice fled. Esmeralda saw their tails whisk out of sight beneath the nearest cupboard.

Fleur was crying again—cowering next to Esmeralda with her eyes shut tight. Esmeralda kept hers open. She watched the custodian approach. He set his lantern on the floor. Its light flashed across her vision and she blinked.

And then Gurkin was staring right at them. Fleur whimpered. Esmeralda felt sick.

The custodian sneered, displaying stained and crooked teeth behind a bristly ginger-colored beard. He picked up the baton and studied it. He scratched his head and looked around. He said, "Hello? Is anyone here?"

Gurkin dropped the baton and reached for the trap, then appeared to change his mind. Abruptly, he stood up, grabbed the lantern, and left the room.

Esmeralda let out a gasp. Conrad and Maksim rushed out from under the cupboard; Gringoire followed close behind. He said, "I think he's gone to get something flat to push under the mousetrap. We've got to get you out before he comes back."

This time the mice moved with precision born of experience. Slowly, the cage rose up.

"You go first," said Esmeralda.

Fleur tried to push herself through the hole at the bottom of the trap. "I can't fit!"

"She needs more room! Shift the weight farther away from the fulcrum!"

By now the mice knew that by *fulcrum*, Gringoire meant the thread spool. The mousetrap tilted up farther. Fleur pushed herself through the hole and began to crawl along the floor toward the outer edge of the mousetrap.

"Stay where you are, everyone!" said Gringoire. "She's almost out from under—"

But someone moved. The mousetrap fell and Fleur gave a scream. "My foot! My foot!"

Madame Giselle wrung her hands. "Oh, Fleur! Oh, my poor, dear Fleur!"

Gringoire shouted, "Lift it up again! Apply more force!"

Slowly, the mousetrap rose up.

"She's out," said Gringoire.

Fleur gave a moan. Her foot was twisted at an odd angle.

"Your turn, Esmeralda!" said Gringoire. "Hurry now!"

Before she could move, however, they heard Gurkin's footsteps. The mice on the lever leaped down, and the trap crashed to the floor. Everyone except Maksim, Conrad, Gringoire, and Fleur rushed to hide under the cupboard.

"Run!" cried Esmeralda, her hands gripping the bars of the mousetrap. "Take Fleur with you!"

Maksim's hands curled around hers. "I don't want to leave you!"

Gurkin was at the door. "You can't help me now. Get away, Maksim!" cried Esmeralda.

He gave her an agonized look and let go.

Gringoire limped toward the cupboard. Maksim and Conrad followed, carrying Fleur between them. Esmeralda saw them reach safety, then shut her eyes as Gurkin's lantern flashed across the room.

She heard the floor creak. Then she heard Gurkin let out a gasp. He must be surprised to see only one mouse in the trap, she thought.

Now she could smell him. She could smell his hands—a dreadful odor of grease and vinegar and *human*—as Gurkin lifted the trap. She was sliding. Her eyes flew open as the custodian shook the trap, and she had to throw herself out of the way of the sharp spikes. He shook the trap again, and Esmeralda slid out the hole in the bottom.

She landed hard. She picked herself up and ran into a metal wall. She turned and ran into another wall. And another! She looked up and saw the custodian's yellow-toothed sneer.

"I got one of you, anyway!" muttered Gurkin.

Then a roof slammed down on her prison, shutting out the light.

CHAPTER 22

Grateful for Turnips

"YOU SHOULD BE GRATEFUL for turnips," Mama told Irina.

Now that Papa was out of work, Mama seemed to make turnip stew more often than not. It was easy to get tired of turnip stew, and being tired of turnip stew sometimes led to complaining. The only good thing about turnips, as far as Irina was concerned, was that they made her think of a story she liked.

One night, she asked Papa to tell it to her at

bedtime. He said, "You're too old for that one. You've heard it a hundred times!" But she insisted, and he told her the story. The characters—a grandfather, a grandmother, their granddaughter, their dog, and their cat—all formed a long chain, all of them trying to uproot an enormous turnip from the garden. Only when a little mouse helped them pull did the turnip pop out of the ground.

The story made Irina think of the dancing mouse. She wondered if the mouse had found the bundle of dresses that she had left under the cupboard, and she went to sleep wishing that she could go to the theater with Mama in the morning. That didn't seem likely; these days, Mama felt that Irina should stay home and keep Papa company.

Then, in the morning, Irina learned that the grocer who had sold Mama the turnips for last night's stew had mentioned that he needed someone to help clean out his storeroom. And Mama had mentioned that Papa could help him. So, Irina didn't have to stay home to keep Papa company, and she went to the theater after all, grateful for turnips and eager to find out what she could about the dancing mouse.

As it happened, what Irina found out alarmed her. No sooner had she and Mama entered the costume department than Madame Federova told them that the custodian had finally caught a mouse in one of his traps.

"Right here in the costume department," said Madame Federova. "No doubt it was one of the mice you brought with you that day, Sonya Borisovna. Just think! They've been lurking here all this time."

Irina said, "Where is the mouse?"

"The custodian has taken it away, thank goodness," said Madame Federova.

Taken it away! To drown it? To poison it? Irina's heart pounded.

She said, "I left Lyudmila in my coat pocket, Mama. May I go get her?"

This wasn't a lie; she *had* left her doll in the cloakroom, but Irina wanted to look for Gurkin on her way back to the costume department.

"Go ahead. But don't dawdle," said Mama, already speaking through a mouthful of pins.

"I won't." This was only a tiny lie. She would be as quick as she could.

In no time at all, Lyudmila was in Irina's pocket.

As for Gurkin, Irina found him in a hallway, talking to the theater director. She ducked into an open doorway to listen to their conversation.

"I assure you, Monsieur, that the rodent we caught last night was an aberration," said Gurkin. "That is to say, these vermin tend to seek shelter indoors in winter, and no doubt that is the case here. Last night's immediate capture of the invader demonstrates that the new traps will continue to be successful. My predecessor, unfortunately, made the error of relying on old-fashioned mousetraps, and—"

Monsieur Vsevolozhsky interrupted Gurkin's babbling. "Just so long as we don't see a repeat of what happened earlier this month. Monsieur Tchaikovsky has been attending many of our rehearsals. I don't want another upset."

"No, sir! I will be disposing of the rodent myself!"

Disposing of . . . Could that mean the mouse was still alive? But where was it?

"Good day, Monsieur," said Gurkin.

The two men parted, and the custodian walked past Irina, even as she pretended to check the lace of her boot. Gurkin was carrying a metal pail with a lid. With sudden, clear conviction, she knew that the mouse was inside the pail. Could it be the dancing mouse?

The custodian began to whistle a tuneless

rendition of the "Dance of the Sugar Plum Fairy."
Irina stood up, ready to follow him, when someone
called, "Is that you, Konstantin Grigorovich?"

The custodian stopped whistling. He looked into
a half-open door on the other side of the corridor.
"What is it?"

"I was hoping to find rags for cleaning. I thought
there were some in this supply room."

Gurkin set the pail down and entered the room.

This was her chance! Irina tiptoed over to
the pail.

She heard the sounds of boxes being moved
around. Gurkin said, "Try the top shelf."

She knelt down and lifted the lid of the pail. A
small gray mouse stared up at her. It was trembling.
There wasn't time to explain or soothe. She had
only a few seconds. Irina scooped up the mouse
with her hand. It was tiny and warm; it squirmed as
she dropped it into the pocket of her pinafore.

She stood up to find Gurkin looming over

her. "What do you think you're doing?" he demanded. He looked into the pail. "Where is the rodent?"

Irina opened her mouth. She was too scared to speak.

Gurkin said, "You took it!"

The other custodian came to the door. It was Yuri Petrovich, whose wife had made the spice cookies. He said, "Well, if it isn't Irina!"

Gurkin said, "This girl has stolen a mouse!"

"Why should she do that, sir?"

"She put it in her pocket!"

"Is there a mouse in your pocket, Irina?" asked Yuri Petrovich.

A tear rolled down Irina's cheek. She bit her lip, fighting back more tears.

"Come now, sir! You've made her cry."

"I tell you, I *saw* her take it! Turn out your pocket, girl!"

Irina wiped her eyes. She turned out her pocket. Lyudmila tumbled to the floor.

"It's just a doll, sir," said Yuri Petrovich. He bent down, picked up Lyudmila, and handed her to Irina.

"Th-thank you," Irina stammered as she put Lyudmila back in her pocket.

Yuri Petrovich said, "I'm sorry about all this. Tell your papa I said hello, yes?"

"May I—may I go?" asked Irina.

Yuri Petrovich nodded, and the last thing Irina heard as she hurried away was Gurkin's voice. "The mouse was right here, I tell you! Right here in this pail!"

Irina returned to the cloakroom, where she knew she would be alone. She had already felt inside her pocket—and found the tiny hole at the bottom of it. Now she closed the door behind her and whispered, "Are you there, mouse?"

Carefully, she lifted her pinafore, revealing her gray woolen dress. The mouse clinging to a fold in the fabric was almost the same color. It jumped to the floor.

Irina knelt down.

The mouse turned and looked up with eyes that were dark and liquid, like drops of ink.

Irina said, "It *is* you, isn't it? You're the dancing mouse!"

CHAPTER 23

Yes, I Can

DON'T BE SCARED! Please don't run away!"
said the girl.

Esmeralda had never wanted to do anything
more in all her life.

At any moment, the girl might reach out with
her enormous hand, which smelled so awfully of
human. She might scoop her up again! She might
grab her around the middle with her grasping
fingers and swing her up into the air!

"I'm sorry I had to pick you up like that. I'm sure *I* wouldn't like it if a giant hand grabbed me. I couldn't do anything else, though. Gurkin was going to—" The girl tilted her head. "Can you understand me?"

There were all kinds of reasons not to answer this question.

When she was a child, Esmeralda had asked her mother, "Why do people set mousetraps? Why do they try to kill us?"

"Humans think we are pests," her mother had explained. "They don't know we like their stories and their music and their ballets. All they know is that we live inside their homes and buildings and eat their food. And, of course, some mice are more careless than others and leave a mess in plain sight; those mice give the rest of us a bad reputation."

"We should tell them that we're not like those mice. We should tell them we're not pests," Esmeralda had argued.

But at that point, her brother had interjected. "Humans don't know we're smart enough to tell them anything, Esmeralda. If they *did* know, they would catch us and put us in cages, just so they could ask us questions and see how we'd answer. They do that with animals, you know. I read about a horse that was foolish enough to reveal that it knew how to count. A man put the horse in a circus and forced it to count in front of thousands of people. He wouldn't feed the horse if it didn't do what he said."

"My name is Irina," said the girl. "Please don't be frightened of me. I've been leaving food for you under the cupboard in the costume department. And I left some dresses for you. Did you find them?"

"Yes," Esmeralda said without thinking. She clapped her hands over her mouth. Suppose Irina should put her in a circus!

"What?" said the girl.

But Irina hadn't understood her. Gringoire had

once explained to Esmeralda that mouse voices were too high for humans to hear properly.

"I hope you found the dresses," said Irina. "I loved watching you dance in my room. I wish I could see you dance again!"

There was a knock at the door of the cloakroom. The door pushed open, and Esmeralda dove for cover behind a pair of boots.

"Who are you talking to, Irina?" Esmeralda recognized Irina's mother's voice. "Come along, now. There isn't as much work as I thought there would be today. We're going home soon."

"But we'll come back?"

"Yes, yes. I'll bring you again."

Esmeralda heard the door close.

She was safe! She was . . .

Late for practice!

Nobody was at the barre when Esmeralda arrived at class. The mice stood talking in small groups. Many of her friends were in tears, and Esmeralda could see Conrad sitting at the far end of the rehearsal space, his head buried in his arms. Gringoire was there, too. And Maksim—dear Maksim!

Madame Giselle was the first to spot her. "Oh, my dear Esmeralda! You are alive!" she cried.

Everyone rushed toward Esmeralda. Maksim had to push his way through a crowd of dancers. He lifted her off the ground in a hug. "I thought you were drowned in the Neva River!"

Conrad and Gringoire came forward, too. Maksim let go of Esmeralda so that her cousin and brother could embrace her. Conrad said, "I can't believe you're here! Maksim and Gringoire came up with a plan to rescue you, but we didn't know where Gurkin had taken you. We were afraid that . . ."

He couldn't go on.

"I'm fine," said Esmeralda. "I'm safe now—"

"What happened to you?" said Gringoire.

"I'll tell you all about it later. But—" Esmeralda looked around. "Where is Fleur? Is she all right?"

"Oh, such a tragedy!" said Madame Giselle. "Fleur's foot is broken. She cannot walk!"

"Oh, no!" said Esmeralda.

"Yes, yes! Poor Fleur," said Madame Giselle. "And poor *us,* as well! She cannot walk, and she cannot dance. We will have to cancel the ballet."

Esmeralda's mouth fell open. Madame Giselle couldn't be serious. She couldn't possibly cancel the new ballet—not when they had costumes and sets and a new scenario. Not when everyone had worked so hard!

"There can be no performance until Fleur's foot is better," said Madame Giselle. And who knows when that will be? Certainly not in time for *Clara and the Mouse King.*"

Esmeralda said, "Can't somebody else take on Fleur's role?"

"Nobody else knows the choreography. No one

else is good enough." Madame Giselle's voice was choked with sorrow.

Conrad said gently, "We're going to have to give up on this production, Esmeralda."

She stared at him in disbelief. The new production wasn't all they would be giving up. Without *Clara and the Mouse King,* the Russian Mouse Ballet Company might not survive. "No!" she said. "No! We're not going to give up! I — *I* know the choreography!"

Everyone fell silent. Madame Giselle and Conrad looked at her without blinking.

Esmeralda's tail twitched. She willed it to lie still and flat on the floor. She said, "I've been practicing in private — Fleur's dances as well as my own. I've been working on keeping my tail in position without the training ribbon, and I think — well, I'm pretty sure — that I can do it."

Madame Giselle looked skeptical.

But Conrad's face lit up. "That's wonderful, Esmeralda! This is the solution we need, Madame!"

The ballet mistress hesitated. She looked carefully at Esmeralda. "I wonder, my dear, if you have thought this through. If you dance the role of Clara, you will be viewed as the company's *prima ballerina*. It will be essential that the audience love your performance. They must admire and adore you. And if they do not . . ."

Esmeralda nodded. She understood what Madame Giselle was telling her: if she failed, if her tail fell out of position, or if she couldn't dance with sufficient emotion, she might very well destroy any chance she had at a career in ballet.

The ballet mistress looked at Esmeralda, holding her gaze. "Can you do this, my dear? Can you make the audience love you on opening night?"

A great part of Esmeralda wanted to cry out that *no*, she couldn't. How could she possibly take on something so difficult? What if she were to fail?

Then Esmeralda thought of her fellow dancers—her friends, rehearsing even when they were hungry, even when they were tired from extra scrounge patrols, even as they lived in terror of a cruel custodian bent on their destruction. They were all looking at her now, waiting to hear what she would say.

She thought of rewriting the scenario for the ballet with her brother and cousin—how excited they had been. She thought of Gringoire and Conrad stealing the sets. She thought of Maksim, helping her to find food—and taking her to the Balalaika Café so that she could dance for an audience. Maksim was looking at her now, nodding to show that he had faith in her ability. Conrad and Gringoire were nodding, too.

Esmeralda thought of Irina donating costumes to the mice—and then saving her from Gurkin. She thought of Irina's last words to her: *I wish I could see you dance again.*

Her head felt light, her throat dry. She hadn't slept . . . she hadn't had anything to drink or eat since—well, she really couldn't remember. She had been caught in a mousetrap, had spent the night in prison, thinking she would be drowned or thrown into a fire, and she had been rescued by a human girl. Esmeralda felt as if she had gone on a long journey and returned somehow braver than before.

Madame Giselle said, "Can you do it, Esmeralda?"

She took a deep breath. "Yes, Madame. Yes, I can."

CHAPTER 24

Battle Scene

"MONSIEUR TCHAIKOVSKY WILL be in the audience today!"

The announcement one afternoon several days later that the great composer would be in the theater caused more than a little excitement among the members of the Russian Mouse Ballet Company. Of course, Monsieur Tchaikovsky would not be watching their small mouse stage. Still, it was inspiring to think of him being so near.

The company would be performing the battle scene in the first act. Rehearsal had not yet started, and the stage was filled with dancers getting themselves ready: the mouse king and his army of mouse soldiers; the evil nutcracker sorcerer and *his* army of toy soldiers. Conrad, wearing a crown made of gold foil appropriated from a box of chocolates from Mademoiselle dell'Era's dressing room, was adjusting his sash. "Full orchestra this afternoon," he commented. "The musicians will be giving it their best, what with the composer being here. You can bet there will be fewer interruptions than usual."

"I suppose you're right," said Esmeralda.

Her cousin must have heard the quaver in her voice. He said, "Oh, Esmeralda! You're not nervous, are you? Madame Giselle and I both think you're going to do fine today! Not just fine—you're going to be fantastic!"

She smiled weakly. She *was* nervous. For the past few days, ever since she had agreed to take on the role of Clara, she had been working in private with Madame Giselle. The ballet mistress had closed the afternoon rehearsals to all the dancers but Conrad, so that Esmeralda could practice the choreography—and practice dancing without the training ribbon. Today would be Esmeralda's first performance with the rest of the ballet company. She said, "I'm relieved it's the battle scene today. Clara has less dancing to do. And no solos!"

She was also relieved that Fleur wouldn't be at rehearsal. Fleur had begun hobbling around with the aid of a crutch fashioned from a twig. She might easily have come to watch—and criticize! But Esmeralda knew from her brother that Fleur was going to sit in the tsar's box today. She and Gringoire were going to watch the human rehearsal. Gringoire was excited because he had heard that the humans were going to fire off a real cannon.

Conrad was struggling with his sash. "Bother! I've put it on too tight again."

"Let me help you."

Her cousin looked around as Esmeralda retied

his sash. Conrad said, "That's odd. I think we've got only about half the dancers we're supposed to have. Do you suppose they didn't get the call for today's rehearsal?"

But Esmeralda was thinking about the cannon. She didn't know exactly how it worked, but she had gathered that there might be an explosion involved. It sounded exciting, and she almost would have preferred to be up in the tsar's box with Gringoire and Fleur.

What happened *was* exciting, though not in the way Esmeralda had expected.

It happened partway into the battle scene.

On the mouse stage, Clara was looking on in terror as the mouse king and his army of mice faced off with the evil nutcracker sorcerer and his army of toy soldiers. On the human stage, the cannon went off with a *crack*!

The crack was followed by a human scream. The

music came to a shrieking halt. There were more screams, and then a giant crash.

On the mouse stage, the nutcracker sorcerer's toothpick wand fell to the floor.

The mice froze, listening to the sound of thundering feet coming from the human stage. And above that sound, screams of real terror.

"What is going on?" said Conrad.

As soon as he could, Gringoire found them and described the scene of catastrophe he had witnessed. "The human stage was crowded with dancers," he said. "People in mouse and soldier costumes and so on. Then the cannon went off—I'm sure you heard that—only a little puff of smoke, by the way. And then, suddenly, Franz showed up with about twenty or thirty mice! Not people in mouse costumes, mind you, but *real* mice. They ran across the stage, making every effort to be seen. And somebody— it might have been that girl playing Clara—"

"Stanislava Belinskaya," said Esmeralda.

"Right! She knocked over the Christmas tree! It's a wonder none of our mice were crushed—or stepped on!"

"Did everyone escape?" asked Conrad.

"Yes, yes! The idiots got away! The whole thing was well planned—I'll give them that much credit. And then Monsieur Ivanov was up on the stage, shouting for everyone to calm down. Unfortunately, his advice didn't have any effect on Tchaikovsky. The composer was in hysterics, scrambling over the backs of the chairs and trying to get out of the auditorium without touching the floor!"

"Oh, dear!" said Esmeralda.

"Meanwhile, Fleur was there beside me, cheering everyone on! It seems that she and Franz planned this whole thing together. Their aim is to have Gurkin fired from his position."

Conrad said, "Instead, Franz has been fired."

"What?" said Esmeralda.

"Didn't you hear? Madame Giselle has suspended him indefinitely from the ballet company. She was furious that an entire rehearsal was upset."

"But Franz wasn't the only mouse involved. What about Fleur?" said Esmeralda. "Surely Madame Giselle didn't fire *her*!"

"I don't think Madame Giselle knows she was involved. And there's no real point to suspending Fleur, since she can't dance anyway. As for the other mice, if they were to be suspended, we wouldn't have enough dancers for *Clara and the Mouse King*."

"Do you think Franz and Fleur's plan worked?" Esmeralda wondered aloud. "Do you really think Gurkin will be fired?"

"I wouldn't be surprised," said her brother. "The question is, at what cost to us mice?"

CHAPTER 25

The Peppermint-Oil Plan

MAKSIM CAME TO THE Mariinsky for supper the next evening. He brought along a feast: an entire mushroom dumpling, a tea cake, and four sugared almonds—one for each mouse.

"It feels like a party!" said Esmeralda.

"It is a party," said Maksim. "We haven't yet celebrated your escape from that monster with the mousetrap."

"Speaking of *that monster*," said Conrad, "Monsieur Vsevolozhsky has indeed fired Gurkin."

"Good-bye and good riddance," said Maksim. "How about some more tea cake, Esmeralda?"

She had already eaten too much, but she took another helping anyway, just to please Maksim. "I can't believe Gurkin is gone!" Esmeralda commented.

Gringoire said, "Monsieur Vsevolozhsky has yet to hire a new chief custodian. Let's just hope that Gurkin's replacement won't be even worse than he was."

With a shudder, Esmeralda recalled what her brother had said about an *electrocuting mousetrap*. She said, "I wish people would stop setting traps for us."

Gringoire sighed. "I couldn't agree more. Mousetraps are bad when we *can't* outwit them, of course—witness what happened to Fleur! But to my mind, mousetraps are almost as bad when we *can* outwit them. As soon as people know we're in the building, they make up their minds that they've got to get rid of us. If they could, they would come after us with cannon fire!"

"People hate us," said Conrad through a mouthful of tea cake.

Esmeralda objected. "Not everyone. Irina likes mice. She rescued me!"

"For which we are grateful," said Gringoire, "but you cannot deny that her father was a setter of mousetraps."

"He might not have set them if Gurkin hadn't been pushing him to do it," said Esmeralda. "I've heard Mikhail Danilovich call us *clever*. I think he admired us!"

Gringoire made a face. "I wish he'd had a different way of showing his admiration. Something less threatening to our lives."

"Like peppermint oil," said Maksim.

They all looked at him.

He said, "They use it in the house where I live to keep us out of the cupboards."

"Doesn't it make you sick?" asked Esmeralda, remembering how the peppermint candy had made her feel.

"Not if we stay away from it. We just find other ways to get in and out of the cupboards. The humans are none the wiser."

Struck suddenly by an idea, Esmeralda sat up straight. "Are you saying that if the custodians at the theater were to use peppermint oil instead of mousetraps, we would all be safe?"

"Certainly—if you stay away from the peppermint oil," said Maksim.

Esmeralda leaned over and gave him a kiss—just behind his whiskers. "That's it!" she said. "If we can convince the custodians to use peppermint oil—*and* if we can convince the mice to stay inside the walls here at the theater—then the humans will think they've chased us out at last. We'll never have to worry about another mousetrap again!"

Conrad scratched the back of his head. "Without mousetraps, how will we get enough food?"

Esmeralda looked to her brother. "Gringoire has already said we won't need to worry about food once mice start paying admission for *Clara and the Mouse King*."

"You have a point," said her brother, "but exactly how are we supposed to make the custodians use peppermint oil?"

Everyone pondered. Maksim said, "Couldn't you just leave some where your custodians will find it? It comes in little bottles. I could bring you one from the house where I live. Modest and Pyotr will help me. It shouldn't be too hard."

Gringoire said, "We could put the bottle on a shelf in the supply room. . . ."

But Esmeralda was shaking her head.

"What's wrong with the supply room?" said Conrad. "The custodians are sure to see the bottle in there."

Esmeralda said, "I think we should leave it where Irina can find it."

"Irina! The girl with the costumes?"

Esmeralda explained. "If we were to leave the bottle of peppermint oil under the cupboard in the costume department, and if we were to wrap it up in my handkerchief, Irina would know that we mice had left it for her to find. She'll want to help us. She'll make sure the custodians use it."

Conrad looked unconvinced. "How can a girl do that?"

Esmeralda didn't know how, but she felt sure that Irina would do all she could.

Maksim shared her conviction. He said, "It seems to me that this girl has already helped you mice quite a lot. I think you should give her a chance to help you again."

CHAPTER 26

The Lucky Handkerchief

"WHERE DID YOU FIND THIS?" said Papa.

He was in his chair in the sitting room at home, his newspaper set aside so that he could examine the small glass bottle Irina had given him.

"I found it in the costume department at the theater," Irina told him. She shifted from one foot to the other, watching as Papa removed the stopper from the bottle and sniffed the contents.

"It's peppermint oil," Irina explained. "Mama says it's used for making candy."

Her father nodded. "That's right. But pepper-mint oil is also used as a mouse repellent."

A thrill ran through Irina. Of course, she had known this morning when she had found the bottle that it must have something to do with mice. Or rather, she had known that it must have something to do with one mouse in particular. She said, "What is a *mouse repellent*?"

Papa said, "It's something you use to keep mice away. You and I like the smell of peppermint oil, but mice don't."

To keep mice away! Why, Irina wondered, would the dancing mouse want her to find a bottle of something that did that? Because she was certain that the dancing mouse must have left the bottle for her to find. Why else would it have been wrapped up in the handkerchief with the embroidered letter *E* and left under the mouse cupboard?

"You know," Papa said, "I thought about using peppermint oil to get rid of the mice at the theater."

"Why didn't you?" asked Irina. "Is it very awful for mice?"

He shook his head. "No, no. In fact, it's quite humane. But Gurkin talked me out of it."

Gurkin again! Everyone at the theater had been talking about him today. At supper, Mama had told Papa the news: how hundreds of mice had run across the stage in the middle of a rehearsal, and how Monsieur Tchaikovsky had suffered another fit of hysterics, and how Monsieur Vsevolozhsky had fired Gurkin.

Now Irina asked, "Why did he talk you out of using it?"

"He said he didn't think it would work," said Papa. "I suppose because he knew it wouldn't kill the mice. It only keeps them away."

Away! Irina was certain the dancing mouse did not want to keep away from the Mariinsky. Perhaps the dancing mouse wanted her to get rid of the peppermint oil.

She took the bottle from Papa and sniffed the contents again. Peppermint was such a nice smell! Then again, mice had very tiny noses: the smell might be too strong for them. She said, "Would this really keep mice away from the theater?"

Papa laughed. "Well, it might keep them away from places we don't want them to go inside the theater. My mother used peppermint oil when I was a boy to keep the mice out of the kitchen."

"Did it work?"

"It depends on your perspective," said Papa. "My father used to tease my mother, telling her she had simply chased the mice up into the attic. And my mother would say, 'As long as they stay out of sight, I don't mind.' She was just like you, Irina. She couldn't bear the thought of hurting little creatures."

Papa returned to his paper. But Irina pushed the stopper into the bottle of peppermint oil and slipped the bottle into her pocket. She was sure she knew exactly what the mouse wanted her to do.

• • •

Papa was helping at the grocer's all that week, so Irina accompanied Mama to the theater again the next morning. The bottle of peppermint oil was in the pocket of her pinafore. So was the embroidered handkerchief. "For good luck," Irina told herself.

Halfway through the morning, she asked if she might go for a walk. "Just inside the theater," said Irina.

Mama was busy stitching gold braid on a soldier costume. "I suppose it's all right," she said, adding her customary warning, "but you mustn't bother anyone."

Irina hoped that what she was about to do wouldn't count as *bothering*. Clutching the good-luck handkerchief in her hand, she made her way to Monsieur Vsevolozhsky's office. She mustered her courage and knocked on the door.

"Enter." The director had a deep and imposing voice.

Irina stepped into his office. There were photographs all over the wall—dancers in various poses. There was Monsieur Petipa's daughter, Marie, wearing the Lilac Fairy costume that Irina had helped to sew.

As for the director, he was sitting at a big desk near the window. He didn't look up, and Irina saw that he was dipping a paintbrush in a glass of dirty water. A wooden box of watercolor paints lay open on his desk.

"Hello?" Irina's voice squeaked like a mouse.

Monsieur Vsevolozhsky looked up. He had a thin official-looking mustache—not a friendly beard like Papa's. And he wore a black monocle that made one eye look bigger than the other—an owl's eye. "Hello!" said the director, sounding as surprised to see Irina as she was to see such an important person using watercolors.

But, of course, it shouldn't surprise her that he was painting. Monsieur Vsevolozhsky had designed many of the costumes for *The Sleeping Beauty* and *The Nutcracker*. Irina had seen his pictures in the costume department.

"May I help you?" Monsieur Vsevolozhsky dropped the paintbrush into the water.

She curtsied. "My name is Irina. My mother works in the costume department."

"Are you lost?"

"No, sir." She fingered the lucky handkerchief. "I—I wanted to talk to you about mice."

The director's eyebrows went up, and he adjusted his monocle. "Sit down!" he said, gesturing toward a chair.

As Irina sat down, she couldn't help but look at the half-finished painting—a picture of a ballerina dressed in colorful rags.

Monsieur Vsevolozhsky's gaze followed hers. "A costume design," he explained. "We will be presenting *Cinderella* next year." Then he added, somewhat pointedly, "A ballet with—er—mice."

He looked at her questioningly. Irina gathered her courage and began. "I—I know there are some mice in the theater."

The director frowned. "A great many mice!"

Irina took the bottle of peppermint oil from her pocket and set it on Monsieur Vsevolozhsky's desk.

"What is this?"

"It's peppermint oil."

The director picked up the bottle, removed the stopper, and sniffed. He wrinkled his nose. Apparently, he did not like the smell.

"Papa says it's a mouse repellent," said Irina. "You spread the peppermint oil in all the places you don't want mice to go, and it keeps them away."

"It seems like a rather—er—simple solution to a big problem," said Monsieur Vsevolozhsky.

"Papa says my grandmother used peppermint oil when he was growing up, to keep the mice out of the kitchen. Papa says he never saw any mice in the kitchen." Irina thought of what else Papa had

said—about the mice moving up to the attic. Where, she wondered, would the mice at the theater go?

Monsieur Vsevolozhsky cleared his throat. "The Mariinsky Theater is hardly a kitchen." His voice was stern, almost indignant.

Tears prickled in Irina's eyes. Hastily, she wiped them away with the lucky handkerchief. Her voice quivered as she said, "But—but—Papa was going to use peppermint oil when he worked here, and—"

Monsieur Vsevolozhsky tilted his head. "Your papa worked here?"

She nodded. "Yes, Monsieur. His name is Mikhail Danilovich Chernov."

Once again, the director's eyebrows went up. Once again, he adjusted his monocle.

Irina hurried on. "I know you think Papa was to blame for the mouse in the costume department, but that wasn't his fault! And the mouse didn't mean to scare anyone. And—and—well, Papa would have used the peppermint oil long ago, only Konstantin Grigorovich Gurkin talked him out of it."

At the mention of Gurkin's name, Monsieur Vsevolozhsky removed his monocle and slipped it into his pocket. He rubbed his forehead as if he had a headache. "Those mice . . ." he began.

"Please, Monsieur," said Irina. "Papa is a very good custodian. And peppermint oil is much better than mousetraps. It's more humane, and—and I know it will work!"

She hoped it would work. She hoped the mice would keep out of sight and that, somewhere inside the theater, her own mouse could go on dancing. Irina glanced down at the handkerchief, at the pink letter *E*.

Monsieur Vsevolozhsky picked up the bottle of peppermint oil again, turning it over and over in his hand. At last he said, "I'll tell you what, Irina. Please ask your papa to come see me. I'd like to talk to him."

"Yes, sir." Did this mean the director was going to give her plan a try?

Monsieur Vsevolozhsky set the bottle of peppermint oil down on his desk. "I'll hold on to this, if that's all right with you."

So he could use it for the mice, thought Irina. "Yes, sir!" She jumped to her feet. "Thank you, sir!" She bobbed in a curtsy.

"Thank you, Irina," said the director. His voice was still deep, but not quite as imposing as before, because now he was smiling.

CHAPTER 27

The Theater Posters

AS THE OPENING OF *Clara and the Mouse King* drew near, Esmeralda spent her days rehearsing. She felt as if she spent her nights dancing as well, for she would often dream that she was on stage. Many of her dreams were happy: the audience would cheer as she whirled across the stage. But not infrequently, her dreams were bad: her tail would come unwound, and the audience and her fellow dancers would stare at her in horror.

"Stage jitters—all part of being a performer," Conrad reassured her when she told him of her nightmares. "You're doing splendidly. Everybody thinks so, and Madame Giselle is beside herself— I've never seen her this happy."

Meanwhile, other preparations for *Clara and the Mouse King* continued apace. Gringoire devised a complicated mechanism for handling the watercolor-painting backdrops. Strings were looped through tiny holes along the top edge of each painting. The strings went up and over nails in the walls high above the stage. By pulling on the ends of the strings, a team of twelve mice could raise and lower each backdrop. Gringoire also suggested that the mice increase the number of candle footlights from three to six. "We'll dazzle the audience," he promised.

And then there were the theater posters.

These were Maksim's idea. "I can tell you that the Saint Petersburg mice like to look at the posters the humans use for their productions," he said. "You'll generate a lot of excitement if you use posters to advertise *Clara and the Mouse King.*"

Using cigarette papers, Gringoire produced dozens of posters. On some he drew Esmeralda dancing in her Clara costume. On others, he drew Conrad in his mouse king costume. And on some, he drew Esmeralda and Conrad dancing together. Maksim made sure the posters were displayed throughout Saint Petersburg. "All the places mice like to go," he told Esmeralda.

One of the posters was displayed just outside the secret entrance to the Balalaika Café. Esmeralda saw it there one evening. Maksim had insisted she come out dancing with him. "No practicing tonight; no hunting for food," he had told her. "Just fun! You need it."

Now, as they stood hand in hand in front of the poster, he said, "What do you think, seeing yourself up there like that?"

Esmeralda stared, her head tilted to one side.

"I know it's me, but I still can't quite believe it. It doesn't feel real!"

He took her arm. "That's because it isn't you! It's Clara! Haven't you said that's who you want to be when you're performing that role?"

Saying just the right thing was one of Maksim's many gifts. Esmeralda smiled, and together they walked into the café, where Nadya, Igor, and Dmitri embraced her warmly.

The music started up, and Esmeralda joined her friends on the dance floor. But it wasn't long before the floor cleared and she was dancing alone with Maksim. She could hear the mice around them clap and count out loud as she performed *fouetté* after *fouetté: thirty, thirty-one, thirty-two, thirty-three* . . . She was so dizzy she thought she might spin right off the floor, but she kept on turning until the ecstatic crowd shouted *forty!*

She finished with a flourish of her tail.

"You see? You are already a star!" said Maksim,

sweeping her up in his arms and whirling her around one final time.

Would the Saint Petersburg mice like her controlled ballet performance as much as they liked her wild dancing at the café? At that moment, Esmeralda felt as if they might. And, as she and Maksim left for home, she stole one more look at the theater poster. Maksim was right, she decided. It really *was* Clara up there on the poster.

On the morning after her visit to the Balalaika Café, Esmeralda caught sight of Irina and her father at the theater. The mice had heard only yesterday that Mikhail Danilovich was to be reinstated as chief custodian. Now, here he was with his daughter, the two of them hard at work removing mousetraps. Better still, Esmeralda could see from the small bottle Irina held in her hand that the peppermint-oil plan had worked.

"Smear it on thick—right where that trap was,

Irina," said Mikhail Danilovich. "We don't want any more mice."

"Maybe they're only hiding, Papa," said Irina.

"They had better stay in hiding if I'm to keep my job."

"They will," said Irina.

"We will," whispered Esmeralda.

It was a promise she was determined to keep . . .

By giving the best performance she possibly could.

CHAPTER 28

Dress Rehearsal

DRESS REHEARSALS AT THE Mariinsky were important events. The tsar himself attended many of them, and rumor had it that he would be watching the dress rehearsal for *The Nutcracker*. Madame Giselle, on the other hand, had always made a practice of banning outside observers from dress rehearsals on the mouse stage. "Too many things can go wrong," she was always saying, and in the case of *Clara and the Mouse King*, her words proved to be true.

Some of the mishaps that occurred during the dress rehearsal were relatively minor. Several children in training ribbons tumbled off the stage during the party scene in the first act. Though nobody was injured, somehow, in the resulting confusion, the dancer playing Drosselmouse completely missed his entrance. Then, during the battle scene, Conrad dropped his toothpick sword. One of the soldiers accidentally kicked it across the stage, and the mouse king had to duel empty-handed when he faced off with the evil nutcracker sorcerer.

But the real disaster occurred after the battle scene.

The raising and lowering of the backdrops required a great deal of coordination, not to mention strength. The stagehands were moving the backdrop for the Silvermouse family's drawing room out of the way when something went horribly wrong. The watercolor painting fell forward onto the stage. The dancers managed to skip out of the way, but the

backdrop knocked over one of the candle footlights, and the edge of the painting caught fire. Fortunately, the quick-acting fire-mice prevented it from going up in flames. But the orchestra was halfway through the second act before the mess was cleaned up.

Gringoire was mortified by the failure of the mechanism he had devised for changing the sets. "I suppose it's better that it should happen now rather than on opening night," he said glumly when the rehearsal was over. "I'll fix the problem so it can't happen again, and we'll have to hope the audience won't notice those scorch marks."

As for Esmeralda, she was relieved that she had made it through the dress rehearsal without making any mistakes.

"A flawless performance, my dear!" said Madame Giselle. "Technically perfect! When we open tomorrow night, you will light up the stage!"

"Thank you, Madame," said Esmeralda, even as she wondered if the ballet mistress was simply trying to be encouraging. The truth was that Esmeralda felt as if something vital had been missing from her performance. Surely Madame Giselle must have noticed.

Esmeralda relayed her concerns to her cousin. To her surprise, he agreed. "Of course Madame Giselle is being encouraging. But don't worry! She knows that what you need is an audience. It will make all the difference in the world."

Was that the answer? If Esmeralda was to believe Maksim, there would be quite a large audience on opening night. "I predict a record crowd," he had told her. "I'll be there, as will Dmitri, Igor, and Auntie Nadya, and all of your fans from the Balalaika Café. But the posters have done their work, too. I can't remember the last time everyone was so excited about a new ballet!"

"Does it make you nervous to dance in front of an audience?" Esmeralda asked Conrad.

"I find it invigorating!" he said. "There's

something about dancing in front of others that makes you want to do your very best."

Esmeralda thought of dancing at the Balalaika Café. It occurred to her that she always felt shy when she first stepped out on the floor. But her cousin was right: her shyness always vanished when she began to dance for the other mice. Just as he said, her performance was stronger for knowing that others were watching.

She thought of the night she had danced for Irina. She would dance for her audience on opening night just as she had then.

Tomorrow night, she would let the music take hold of her, and she would become Clara.

CHAPTER 29

Opening Night

RATS HAD NEVER COME to see a Russian Mouse Ballet Company production before, so it caused quite a commotion among the Mariinsky mice when two of them showed up for the opening-night performance of *Clara and the Mouse King*.

The mouse dancers gathered backstage were all abuzz, wondering if the rats had come to cause trouble.

"No!" Esmeralda told them. "Modest and Pyotr are friends of mine."

Conrad further calmed their fears. "The Saint Petersburg mice in the audience don't mind Esmeralda's friends, so why should we? Besides, you should see what they paid for admission—bread and cheese that will last a week for one of our families!"

Conrad told Esmeralda, "Maksim was right. We're going to have a packed house tonight!"

"Is he here?" asked Esmeralda. "Have you seen Maksim?" She felt a moment of panic. Suppose something should prevent him from coming!

Her cousin grinned. "He's sitting in the front row with three of your fans."

"Dmitri and Igor and Nadya." It was a comfort to know that they were here with Maksim.

Conrad said, "Listen! I think Gringoire's about to begin!"

Esmeralda's brother liked to serve as master of ceremonies for the ballet company's productions, using a device that he called a speaking trumpet.

This was nothing more than a rolled-up paper cone, but when Gringoire shouted into the small end, his voice could be heard by everyone in the audience.

Now, in his best master-of-ceremonies voice, Gringoire began. "Welcome, my friends, to the most exciting night ever for the Russian Mouse Ballet Company! As I am sure you are aware, this evening's performance marks the premiere of a new ballet with music composed by none other than Pyotr Ilyich Tchaikovsky. Those of us who loved *The Sleeping Beauty* are thrilled that Russia's renowned composer has provided yet another fantastic score."

There was a smattering of applause.

Gringoire continued. "Tonight, the Russian Mouse Ballet Company is proud to present its own production. The ballet that you will see tonight, *Clara and the Mouse King*, is a story written by mice, about mice, and for mice!"

The applause was louder this time, and Conrad squeezed Esmeralda's hand. "This is it!" he murmured. "This is what we've been waiting for!"

Yes, this was the night they had worked for! Esmeralda could hear the pride in Gringoire's voice as he went on with his speech: "As you can already see from the scenery behind me, this performance marks the first time ever that the Russian Mouse Ballet Company will have stage sets. And I know that many of you have heard rumors—and I am here to confirm them—that tonight, our dancers will be wearing costumes."

Esmeralda smoothed the skirt of the pink dress with crystal beads. She could scarcely believe that she was wearing the costume that Fleur would have worn. In fact, Fleur had insisted upon it. "I just want to make sure that *Clara and the Mouse King* is a success," she had told Esmeralda, adding, "I want to make sure there's a ballet company for me to come back to when I can dance again." Fleur would be watching tonight from the front row, with Madame Giselle sitting beside her.

Gringoire continued. "As for tonight's performers, I know you will be pleased that the role of the mouse king will be filled by the inimitable Conrad . . ."

Esmeralda's brother had to wait for the applause to subside.

"And I know that you will be saddened to hear that our own Fleur de Lys is unable to dance tonight because of an injury . . ."

Quite a few mice applauded this announcement. Esmeralda knew that Fleur wouldn't be happy about that.

"But we are delighted to introduce the Russian Mouse Ballet Company's rising new star, Esmeralda, in the role of Clara."

She jumped to hear her name shouted out. She jumped again to hear the applause her name generated. She was grateful to Conrad, who squeezed her hand again. "You'll be great," he told her, even as there came a much louder burst of applause.

It came from the human audience in the large theater. The orchestra conductor, Monsieur Drigo, had come out to the podium. *The Nutcracker* was about to begin.

"And so we present to you *Clara and the Mouse King*!" shouted Gringoire.

Madame Giselle had spoken at length about the importance of the first scene. "From the moment Clara appears, I want everyone to know that *she* is the star of this ballet. The audience must fall in love with Clara even before the mouse king does."

Did the audience love her? Esmeralda couldn't be sure. She was so nervous when she entered the stage that she nearly missed a step. But her hours of practice paid off, and she didn't lose her equilibrium. Her confidence increased as she realized she was dancing at least as well as she had at the dress rehearsal.

Trumpets heralded the entrance of the mouse king. His Majesty and his entourage paraded grandly around the stage, and Esmeralda concentrated on becoming Clara—on being aware that the mouse king had noticed her, and that he wanted to dance with her.

And, of course, that she wanted to dance with him.

Soon all the party guests were dancing. The couples traded partners as they promenaded about the stage. The mouse king and Clara touched hands, then parted—their gazes lingering on each other. When the children in their colorful ribbon sashes took over and the adults drew back to watch them dance, Esmeralda stole a look at the audience. She couldn't see far beyond the candle footlights, but she thought she saw Igor in the first row.

Oh, dear! Was her friend yawning?

The music grew sinister, and Esmeralda snapped back to attention. Drosselmouse, wearing a black ribbon sash and an eye patch, had arrived at the party. Madame Giselle's choreography called for Clara to escape Drosselmouse's unwanted advances by dancing from one group of party guests to another. She was looking for the king. Unfortunately, His Majesty had been pulled away by one of his courtiers. When Drosselmouse presented Clara's little brother, Fritz, with a Christmas present of some life-size and very dangerous-looking toy soldiers (mice dressed in black military sashes), Clara tried to warn her parents. And when the leering Drosselmouse presented Clara with a life-size leering nutcracker, she drew back in alarm.

Seeing her distress, the mouse king came to her rescue. Swords were drawn, and Drosselmouse was ousted from the party.

The mouse king comforted Clara and gave her *his* present: a bouquet of life-size dancing violets played by several of Esmeralda's friends from the *corps de ballet*.

The dance of the violets was charming, but to Esmeralda's ears, the applause that followed it seemed unenthusiastic. She stole another look at the audience. Igor was shifting in his seat. He wasn't even looking at the stage! His eyes were closed!

Esmeralda now thought of something else Madame Giselle had said: "The audience must feel Clara's fear of Drosselmouse and his gift. They must feel relief when the mouse king rescues her."

Had the audience felt Clara's fear? Did they feel relieved? It alarmed Esmeralda that she couldn't tell. She was so used to having the crowd at the Balalaika Café respond to her performances. Once, when dancing to a particularly sad song, she had brought Nadya to tears! Another time, when dancing a comical dance, she had made Dmitri and Igor laugh out loud!

It was time for Clara's first *pas de deux* with the mouse king. There would be a longer *pas de deux* in the second act, but that did not mean that this dance could not be just as romantic. Esmeralda took Conrad's hand and concentrated again on becoming Clara—on listening to the music and dancing perfectly.

Conrad lifted her into the air. He set her down, and Esmeralda took a few steps forward. Conrad lifted her again, and together they moved across the stage. Every part of the dance was designed to build the feeling that Clara and the mouse king were meant to be together. And yet, as their *pas de deux* came to an end, Esmeralda knew that she and Conrad had failed. The applause was polite, but nothing more.

Her heart sank. Was it her dancing? How *could* it be? She had kept her tail in position the entire time. She had danced flawlessly. She had danced with emotion . . .

Or had she?

Had she truly *felt the music* in the same way she did when she danced at the Balalaika Café?

Esmeralda knew that she had not.

She was distracted tonight — more concerned about the reaction of the audience than about what she was feeling. She had been so concerned about dancing flawlessly, so worried about keeping up with the music, that she had forgotten how to let it flow through her. And as for playing a role — she had felt less like Clara and more like Esmeralda trying to feel like Clara. She was no better than Fleur if that was all she could do!

It was altogether the wrong time to have such a realization. She was in the middle of a performance. The party guests were leaving. The mouse king was leaving, and she was about to be alone on the stage. It would be up to her to entertain an audience that might very well be bored enough to leave at intermission.

The music became soft and quiet. It was nighttime, and the Silvermouse family had gone to bed.

All except Clara, who lingered behind. She purposefully ignored Drosselmouse's gifts—the hideous nutcracker and the army of toy soldiers. Instead, Clara tiptoed across the stage toward the mouse king's gift. The violets began to dance, and Clara danced with them.

The clock struck midnight.

The flowers wilted and fell to the floor, dead.

The nutcracker jerked his limbs and came to life. He pulled a magic wand from his sash and pointed it right at Clara.

A sorcerer! The audience let out a collective gasp. Was it because they were frightened for Clara? Or was it because, as she shrank back from the nutcracker sorcerer, Esmeralda let her tail unwind? It wasn't by accident, though Esmeralda knew that Madame Giselle would think that it *was*. Madame Giselle would think she had committed the worst possible error.

Maybe she had. But what other choice was there?

The nutcracker sorcerer dragged Clara across the stage. Clara's tail whipped back and forth—as Esmeralda's tail had done when she had tried to escape from Sasha.

A ballerina must not make noise, but she could call for help with her dancing. Clara now began calling for help, reaching out with her arms. *Help me!* she implored.

A moment later, the mouse king and his army leaped onto the stage. The nutcracker sorcerer threw Clara aside, lifted his wand, and cast a spell. In an instant, the toy soldiers sprang to life.

The two armies fell into battle. Clara joined in, dodging back and forth, dancing around the soldiers. With her tail unfurled, she could turn faster and leap higher than anyone else. The nutcracker sorcerer's soldiers had to fall back as she whirled through their midst.

The nutcracker sorcerer raised his wand, ready to strengthen his spell.

Clara pulled off an imaginary slipper and hurled it at him.

She missed!

The nutcracker sorcerer picked up the imaginary slipper and threw it back. It knocked Clara in the head, and she stumbled and fell. "Oh, no!" cried a voice from the audience.

Lying on the floor, pretending to be unconscious, Esmeralda felt a mix of satisfaction and hope. She had made *somebody* care about the story.

But what would Madame Giselle think? The ballet mistress's choreography had called for Clara to look frightened during the battle, to watch from the side until the moment she threw her slipper at the nutcracker sorcerer. Clara was not supposed to join in the fight.

But Clara *would* fight, Esmeralda told herself. She would want to protect the mouse king.

Now the music grew somber. The mouse king

had been defeated; his soldiers were carrying their wounded leader off the stage. Murmurs of concern rippled through the audience even as the magical notes of a harp brushed the air.

Clara opened her eyes. She rose to a sitting position. The nutcracker sorcerer stood over her, waving his wand. The audience hissed in unison as he worked his evil enchantment on Clara—making her stand up, manipulating her like a puppet. He waved his wand, and Clara's head dipped sleepily. Her tail was listless. The nutcracker sorcerer was making her forget the mouse king.

Behind the sorcerer, the stagehands were changing the scenery. At dress rehearsal, this had been the moment when the backdrop had fallen forward and caught fire. Now, Esmeralda wondered if dancing with her tail out of position might become an even worse disaster.

But only for a moment: then she was Clara

again. The nutcracker sorcerer waved his wand, and she turned slowly around, staring in wonder as snowflakes drifted onto the stage. The nutcracker sorcerer lifted his wand and made Clara dance with them.

It was cold in the snowy forest, and as Clara danced, she forgot who she was. The nutcracker sorcerer worked his enchantment, and Clara forgot that she loved the mouse king. She was a snowflake spinning through the air.

The music worked its enchantment, too, and Esmeralda forgot about the audience. She forgot about Madame Giselle. All she wanted was to dance — to feel the melody in her arms and her legs and . . . her tail. She was Clara, lost in a snowstorm.

Until she danced off the stage.

Then, suddenly, in the dim light behind the backdrop, in the hush that followed the last note of music, Clara became Esmeralda. The snowflakes surrounding her were the dancers in the *corps de ballet*—her friends, dressed in white lace gowns.

They were all staring at her.

Esmeralda opened her mouth to speak—to explain—to apologize—

But her words were drowned out by applause.

CHAPTER 30

Because of Irina

*E*SMERALDA?"

She turned around.

Her cousin, his gold-paper crown still askew from the battle, was making his way through the crowd of snowflake-costumed ballerinas.

"Conrad!" Esmeralda threw her arms around him. "I danced with my tail out of position!"

"I know!"

She was close to tears. "I couldn't think of what else to do! I thought the audience was going to leave!"

Conrad pulled away. "Where did you learn to dance like that? The way you performed those *pirouettes* in the 'Waltz of the Snowflakes'—I've never seen anyone turn so quickly."

"Madame Giselle must be furious!" said Esmeralda.

Conrad didn't seem to hear her. "And those leaps you performed during the battle!"

"I know I shouldn't have joined in the fight. But I felt like I *had* to fight. Clara wouldn't have stood by and done nothing—"

Again, Conrad didn't seem to hear. "I would swear you made two full turns in the air when you performed that *saut de basque*!"

"Three turns," said Esmeralda. "I know I shouldn't have done it, but—"

"Shouldn't have done it! What are you talking about? The audience loved it! They're still clapping!"

"Esmeralda!"

This time the voice that called her name was

sharp and angry. Esmeralda turned around to find herself face-to-face with Madame Giselle.

"What happened to you?" the ballet mistress demanded. "You danced perfectly all through the first scene. And then—I do not know *what* you were doing! Did you forget the choreography?"

"I'm sorry, Madame!"

"Your tail was waving about like a piece of string!"

Esmeralda's stomach dropped. "I know! I'm truly sorry! But I was just so desperate to—"

"To what?" Madame Giselle interrupted. "To destroy your career? To destroy our company?"

"Don't be ridiculous!"

Madame Giselle turned around. Fleur, balancing on her crutch, had come backstage. She glared at the ballet mistress. "Did you see how high Esmeralda leaped? Did you see how fast she turned? Listen to the audience! They *loved* her performance!"

The audience was *still* clapping.

Fleur went on. "I tell you, Madame Giselle, that

once my foot has healed, *I* want to dance the way Esmeralda did tonight."

"But—but it isn't ballet!" said Madame Giselle.

"It's ballet for mice!" said Conrad. "It's something completely new! Something completely *wonderful*! We all need to learn how to dance ballet with our tails."

Madame Giselle didn't speak. She was listening to the audience. They were clapping in rhythm, chanting the same thing over and over.

Conrad nudged Esmeralda. "They're calling for you. They want you to take a bow."

"I can't!" She was trembling, trying to take in what she was hearing. Had she ruined the ballet or saved it?

Conrad put his arm around her. "Don't worry. You don't need to go out there just yet. But you've got to pull yourself together. Intermission will be over soon."

"I quite agree," Madame Giselle said. "You can't fall apart now, not after you've put the audience into such a *state*. Come, Fleur, let's reclaim our seats."

But Fleur had one more thing to say. "Promise that you'll teach me how to dance like that, Esmeralda."

Dazed, Esmeralda nodded.

When they were gone, Conrad turned to her. "You know what you've got to do, don't you?" he asked.

She looked at her cousin with wide, questioning eyes. "I—I don't know."

Conrad grinned. "Give it everything you've got in the second act. Tail and all!"

Esmeralda's favorite part of the night came near the end of the ballet. Clara was safe at last. The mouse king had come to rescue her from the nutcracker sorcerer and his sister, the evil Peppermint Fairy. The citizens of the Kingdom of Sweets, freed from the oppressive rule of the wicked brother and sister, had performed a waltz so beautiful that even the flowers joined in. The mouse king and Clara had danced together. The mouse king had performed a dance for Clara, and now it was her turn to dance for him.

Slowly, carefully, Esmeralda raised her arms, waiting for the magical bell-like tones of the celesta. Her feet took the first tentative, mincing steps, and she tiptoed across the stage.

The audience let out a collective sigh of pleasure. Surely this was music composed for a dancing mouse!

Esmeralda thought of Irina then. She had danced these same steps in Irina's room. If only Irina were here to see her now!

She thought of Irina again at the end of the ballet, when the roar of applause was so overwhelming that she nearly forgot how to curtsy.

Fortunately, Conrad was there to take her hand.

Together, they and the rest of the ballet company acknowledged the audience. And Esmeralda received two tributes—a bouquet of tiny white flowers, and a red rosebud that was nearly as large as she was.

"Oh, Irina!" she murmured. "If only you could see our ballet!"

The white flowers were from Nadya, Igor, and Dmitri; the rose was from Maksim. "We found them in a bouquet at the house where I live," Maksim told Esmeralda. "Auntie Nadya says that if you dry the flowers, they'll keep forever."

Maksim had stayed after the performance to celebrate with Esmeralda, Conrad, and Gringoire. They were in the attic, enjoying a feast of sugared almonds and cake. "A bit of the take from the box office," as Esmeralda's brother put it.

"The perfect end to a perfect night!" said Esmeralda.

Maksim said, "I wish I could have brought some champagne. Next time, maybe!"

"Next time!" said Esmeralda. "To think that there *will* be a next time makes me so happy!"

"Igor, Dmitri, and Auntie Nadya have already told me they plan to see every performance," said Maksim. "And they aren't the only mice who want to see *Clara and the Mouse King* again and again. You can expect more rats in the audience as well, once Modest and Pyotr spread the word."

"Our troubles are over," said Gringoire.

Conrad chuckled. "Unless Esmeralda gets tired of dancing."

"Never!" said Esmeralda.

Of course, who knew what would happen once Fleur's foot was healed? Fleur was a determined competitor. She would learn to dance with her tail, and she wouldn't easily give up her role as *prima ballerina*.

But Esmeralda was surprised to discover that

she didn't mind. The important thing was that she and Fleur *would* be able to compete with each other. The important thing was that the Russian Mouse Ballet Company would survive. And for that, she was grateful.

She thought of Irina again. She said, "We owe so much to her!"

"To whom?" said Conrad.

"To Irina! She gave us the costumes! She saved me from Gurkin. And she helped us get rid of the mousetraps."

"It's true," Gringoire acknowledged. "Irina had as much to do with tonight's success as any of us."

Maksim was studying Esmeralda. "What plan are you hatching, *zvezda moya*?"

My star . . . Esmeralda smiled to hear Maksim use this term of endearment. And it pleased her that he knew her well enough to read her excitement. She said, "I was thinking that we could dance for

Irina. It would be the perfect way to thank her for being so kind to us."

Gringoire said gently, "I don't see how that's possible."

Conrad added, "Even if our stage weren't hidden behind a wall, none of the mice in the company would want to perform for a human. They would be too frightened."

Esmeralda said, "We wouldn't dance for her at the theater. What if we take the ballet to Irina's house?"

Her brother and cousin stared at her.

Esmeralda continued in a rush. "We could go at night when her parents are asleep. Just the two of us, Conrad! We could perform the *grand pas de deux* from the second act. It's the best part of the ballet, and she would see us wearing the costumes she made, and—"

"That's a crazy idea!" said her cousin. "How

would we get there? I think you were lucky last time that Mikhail Danilovich didn't catch you riding inside his coat hem. I think he might notice if there were two of us in there!"

"Three of us," said Maksim. "You can bet I'll come along."

Gringoire gave a polite cough. "Even if you did manage to get there safely, what about the family cat?"

Esmeralda's heart sank. Why were her plans always so fraught with problems?

Then she caught Maksim's eye. He was looking thoughtful. "What did you say the cat's name was?" he asked.

"Sasha. Why?"

He nodded. "If we can find a way to get into Irina's house, then I'm pretty sure I can take care of Sasha."

Esmeralda's heart lifted again. She looked at her cousin. "Think of everything we've done so far,

Conrad. The new scenario, the costumes and the stage sets, the peppermint-oil plan . . . We are every bit as clever as Irina's father says we are. I'm sure we can find a way to sneak into his house and dance for Irina!"

CHAPTER 31

Christmas Morning

IRINA OPENED HER EYES. She stared up at the dark rectangle of her bedroom ceiling and felt her dreams slip away. How cozy it was in her bed!

She yawned and woke up a little more, remembering with pleasure that it was Christmas Eve. Or it might not be Christmas Eve anymore. Perhaps it was already Christmas morning! Papa had been able to buy a Christmas tree after all. If it weren't so cold outside her bed, she could tiptoe out to the sitting room to look at it—like Clara in *The*

Nutcracker. Papa and Mama had finally taken her to see a matinée performance. Afterward, she had visited Mademoiselle dell'Era in her dressing room, and the ballerina had given her a red rose from one of her bouquets. Mama was drying it so Irina could keep it forever.

As she lay there, Irina gradually became aware of a soft, lapping noise. She rolled over on her side and looked down. She murmured, "Sasha?"

The cat was crouched at the edge of a patch of moonlight on the floor near the bed. She was eating something: that was the noise. Irina wrinkled her nose at the sudden strong smell of fish. Then she gasped.

Sasha was not alone. A charcoal-colored mouse with a scar beneath its eye was standing right next to her, but the cat didn't seem to notice or care. She just went on eating.

The mouse looked up at Irina and waved.

She drew in her breath. Was she dreaming?

The mouse turned and beckoned. Looking toward the door of her room, Irina saw two small shapes on the floor. More mice! She thought of *The Nutcracker*—of Clara and the mice in the middle of the night.

The mice ran toward her bed. When they reached the patch of moonlight, Irina gasped again. One of them was her dancing mouse; she knew it must be, for the mouse was wearing Lyudmila's pink dress. The other mouse wore a red ribbon sash over its shoulder and around its middle, and a gold crown that shone in the moonlight. They looked up at her; the dancing mouse curtsied, and the mouse wearing the sash took a bow.

Irina sat up—to prove that she wasn't dreaming. She glanced at her bookshelf. Lyudmila was sitting up, too—staring straight ahead with the serene expression she always wore. Lyudmila couldn't help looking perpetually calm, but Irina was sure that she must be amazed nonetheless.

She looked back at the mice. The charcoal-colored mouse—the one standing next to Sasha, who was *still* busy eating her fish—grinned at her, then gestured toward the other mice, as if to say, *Just watch!*

The mouse wearing the sash took the hand of the mouse wearing the dress. Together, they bowed and curtsied again, just as if they were on the stage at the Mariinsky Theater and acknowledging the applause of their audience.

"I'm the audience," Irina whispered softly.

Joy rose up inside her like a fountain.

But she didn't clap her hands. She didn't want to frighten the mice. Instead, Irina showed her pleasure with a nod, the way Papa said the tsar did sometimes from his box above the Mariinsky stage.

The mice looked at each other. The mouse wearing the dress gave her own tiny nod, and the mice began to dance.

There was no music, but Irina soon guessed

that she was watching the *grand pas de deux* from the second act of *The Nutcracker*. At the matinée performance, Mademoiselle dell'Era and Pavel Gerdt had danced the roles of the Sugar Plum Fairy and her consort. Irina supposed that her own dancing mouse must be the Sugar Plum Fairy. How graceful she was — right to the very tip of her tail, which arced and curled as the dancing mouse leaped and twirled across the floor. From her movements, it was easy for Irina to imagine the music from the ballet.

And yet, it seemed to her that this tiny *pas de deux* was different from what she had seen on the Mariinsky stage. Every time the male mouse lifted the dancing mouse into the air, his gaze followed her. Every time he set her down, his touch lingered. And when the dancing mouse danced away from her partner, he followed her with arms outstretched. It was almost as if the mice were telling a different story from the one she had seen at *The Nutcracker*.

The mice were telling a story that was more romantic.

At the Mariinsky, Irina's favorite part of the *grand pas de deux* had been the variation in which the Sugar Plum Fairy danced alone. She had loved watching Mademoiselle dell'Era dance on her toes. But she loved watching the dancing mouse even more. It didn't matter that there wasn't any music, because Irina could see the melody in the way the mouse tiptoed and twirled across the floor. It was as if the crystalline tones of the celesta had been translated into movement. And after the variation, when the dancing mouse joined again with her partner, and they danced together and he lifted her up into the air, Irina let out a sigh. "Oh," she whispered as the mice took their bows. "Oh, that was wonderful!"

Whether they understood her, she couldn't tell. The two performers continued to curtsy and bow, even as they backed toward the door of her room. They gave a wave before turning and disappearing into the kitchen. The charcoal-colored mouse gave Irina a salute and hurried after the other two.

Irina closed her eyes, holding on to the moment. When she opened them again, she looked at Lyudmila. "You saw them, didn't you?" she whispered.

The doll's smile was as serene as ever.

Irina looked down. To her surprise, Sasha was gone. A fish skeleton lay on the carpet.

Irina slid out of bed.

Sasha was not in the kitchen. Irina hurried past the cold stove and into the sitting room. The cat was up on the windowsill, staring intently at the street outside.

The mice must be safe. Irina sighed with relief. "What do you see, Sasha?" she asked.

The door to her parents' bedroom creaked open. Mama emerged, looking sleepy. Papa came out, too. He said, "Merry Christmas, Irinushka. Can't you sleep?"

"No! I—"

Irina reached the window. She pushed aside the lace curtain. But there was nothing to see outside—only shadows on the snow-covered street.

"Dreaming about mice again, eh?" said Papa.

"Yes," said Irina. "Only it wasn't a dream! Sasha was eating a fish, and I woke up, and there were mice in my room, and they danced, and . . ." Irina looked outside again. She couldn't see any mice, but that didn't mean they weren't there. Papa always said that mice could slip in and out of buildings through the tiniest of cracks.

Her father yawned and stretched his arms. "It's almost time to get up, I think. What do you say, Mama? Shall we have Christmas morning a bit early this year?"

Papa lit the candles on the tree. Mama filled Sasha's saucer. "Cream, not milk, for you on Christmas morning," she told the cat.

They opened their presents. Irina had made handkerchiefs for her parents. Mama's had purple violets embroidered on it. "My favorite flower," said Mama.

"What's this on mine?" Papa wondered aloud.

"It's a broom," said Irina. "To show that you are the world's best custodian."

As for Irina, she had almost as many presents as the children in *The Nutcracker*. There was a sewing basket all her own, filled with needles and pins and spools of colored thread, scissors, a measuring tape, and ribbons, beads, and scraps of fabric for making doll dresses.

"Madame Federova helped me put it together," said Mama.

There was also a new wooden doll the same size as Lyudmila, only with yellow hair and a slightly mischievous expression. Irina decided to name her Clara. She would be Lyudmila's sister.

But the best present of all was a miniature

wooden stage. Papa had made it for her, and Mama had sewed curtains out of real velvet and trimmed them with gold braid. "We thought your dolls might like to dance in a ballet," said Mama.

Irina drew apart the curtains and peered into the tiny stage. It was just the right size for Lyudmila and her new sister. For that matter, it was just the right size for mice.

It was then that Irina noticed a tiny scroll of paper lying on the floor of the stage. When she unrolled it, her eyes widened at the sight of a pencil drawing of her very own dancing mouse—wearing Lyudmila's dress. There were words to read as well:

the RUSSIAN MOUSE BALLET COMPANY

presents Esmeralda in

Clara and the Mouse King

A Ballet in Two Acts

Music by P. I. Tchaikovsky

"It's a ballet poster!" Irina murmured. So Papa had been right in guessing that the mice had their own company.

"*E* for Esmeralda!" Irina thought of the handkerchief with the embroidered letter *E*.

As for *Clara and the Mouse King*, Irina considered the *pas de deux* she had just seen—more romantic than the *pas de deux* in *The Nutcracker*, yet so clearly danced to the same music she had heard at the Mariinsky. Perhaps *she* had been right about *The Nutcracker;* the mice hadn't liked the story. They had come up with one of their own—a story that mice would like.

Papa said, "You look happy, Irinushka."

She looked up at him. "I am happy."

"Because it's Christmas?"

"Yes, and . . ." Irina thought of Esmeralda. Maybe the mouse was home already—back at the Mariinsky Theater. What was she doing right now? Getting ready for her next performance? Or maybe . . .

"Papa," said Irina, "do you think that mice celebrate Christmas?"

Mama clucked her tongue. "Mice again!"

But Papa considered her question. He said, "I can't say as I know. I take it you mean our friends at the theater."

Our friends. Irina liked the sound of that. She nodded.

"Well," said Papa, "I guess mice should be allowed to celebrate if they like. But mind you . . ." He grinned. "They had better stay out of sight!"

Scenario

ACT I

The Silvermouse family — father, mother, their daughter,
Clara, and her brother, Fritz — are having a Christmas party.
The most important guest is the mouse king. Clara greets the
king by performing a dance. The two fall in love at first sight
and dance together.

Another guest, a mouse called Drosselmouse, gives
Clara's brother some toy soldiers. His present for Clara is
a life-size nutcracker, but she finds Drosselmouse and his
gift disturbing. The mouse king comes to her aid, and he
and Drosselmouse fight with swords. The mouse king ousts
Drosselmouse from the party, then gives Clara his present:
some life-size dancing violets.

After everyone leaves the party, Clara admires her present
from the mouse king. At first the flowers dance for her. When
the clock strikes midnight, they wilt, and Drosselmouse's
nutcracker comes to life as an evil sorcerer. The nutcracker
sorcerer tries to kidnap Clara. Hearing her cries for help, the
mouse king and his army come to rescue her. The nutcracker
sorcerer uses magic to turn Fritz's toy soldiers into an army.

A battle ensues, and Clara is knocked out cold. The mouse king is wounded, and his army bears him away to safety.

The nutcracker wakens Clara and enchants her into a state of forgetfulness. He leads her into a snowy pine forest that lies on the border of his kingdom.

ACT II

The nutcracker sorcerer takes Clara to the magical Kingdom of Sweets, over which he rules with his sister, the wicked Peppermint Fairy. The nutcracker sorcerer wants to make Clara his bride. He and his sister enthrall Clara by means of magical entertainments, but the mouse king, recovered from his wounds, returns with his army. In a decisive battle, the mouse king triumphs over the nutcracker sorcerer and the Peppermint Fairy. Clara wakes from her spell and remembers that she loves the mouse king. The citizens of the Kingdom of Sweets rejoice that their evil rulers have been defeated. The ballet comes to a happy end as everyone celebrates the marriage of Clara and the mouse king.

Author's Note

The Nutcracker had its first performance in December 1892 at the Mariinsky Theater in Saint Petersburg, Russia. If you could travel back in time to watch that performance, you would see some of the characters from this book: student ballerina Stanislava Belinskaya performing the role of Clara, Italian ballerina Antonietta dell'Era dancing the role of the Sugar Plum Fairy, and Italian conductor Riccardo Drigo directing musicians playing the score composed by Pyotr Ilyich Tchaikovsky.

That first production was a collaboration between Ivan Alexandrovich Vsevolozhsky, director of the Imperial Theaters of Russia, and the Mariinsky's ballet master Marius Petipa. They based the scenario very loosely on a

French adaptation (by Alexandre Dumas) of *The Nutcracker and the Mouse King*, a story written in 1816 by German author E. T. A. Hoffmann. Hoffmann's marvelous tale has a plot full of twists and turns. If you read his story and then watch a modern production of *The Nutcracker*, you may be astonished at how little of Hoffmann's creation has made its way into the ballet. Nevertheless, one thing *The Nutcracker* and *The Nutcracker and the Mouse King* share in common is mice. Angry mice, led by a mouse king bent on destruction.

Were there mice living in the Mariinsky Theater in 1892? Who can say for sure? One of the great joys of writing is making things up. In the case of *The Nutcracker Mice*, my task has been to imagine what a troupe of dancing mice living at the theater would think of a ballet that casts them in a very bad light—to imagine how they might feel, and to figure out what they might do.

Acknowledgments

In telling the story of *The Nutcracker Mice*, I have had the help of a number of people to whom I am extremely grateful. First and foremost, thank you to my editor, Kaylan Adair, who always asks the right questions about a manuscript. One of my favorite things in the world is working with her to come up with answers to those questions. Another favorite thing is seeing my words illustrated, and what a delight it has been to see Brett Helquist's wonderful drawings. Thank you as well to Lisa Rudden, Chris Paul, and Jessica Saint Jean for all the work they have done to make *The Nutcracker Mice* such a beautiful book, and to copyeditors Kate Schwartz and Maggie Deslaurier for making sure that the language is polished.

I have never taken a ballet class in my life, so I am grateful to Alexandra Koltun, Alex Lapshin, and their talented students at Koltun Ballet Boston for allowing me to watch a ballet class and some truly amazing performances. Thank you also to ballerina Emily Nguyen (a former Clara in her city's production of *The Nutcracker*) for reviewing the ballet passages in *The Nutcracker Mice*.

I am grateful to agents Nancy Gallt and Marietta Zacker for their support and to my writing friends Sarah Goodman, Holly Hartman, Jessica Holland, Kitty Martin, Lisa Phillips, Samuel Valentino, Lynne Weiss, Frankie Wright, and Marlena Zapf for providing encouragement, helpful suggestions, and inspiration. And, as always, thank you to my family. My life as a writer is never a lonely one, and for that I am truly thankful.

KRISTIN KLADSTRUP is the author of the middle-grade novels *The Book of Story Beginnings* and *Garden Princess,* as well as the picture book *The Gingerbread Pirates.* She lives with her family near Boston.

BRETT HELQUIST has illustrated numerous books for children, including *Roger, the Jolly Pirate*; *Chasing Vermeer* and its sequels, by Blue Balliett; and *Martina & Chrissie: The Greatest Rivalry in the History of Sports* by Phil Bildner. He is also the illustrator of the Series of Unfortunate Events books by Lemony Snicket. Brett Helquist lives in New York.